# OUT
# WITH
# LANTERNS

**ALISHA 'PRITI' KIRPALANI**

Readomania

Readomania Publishing
A division of Kurious Kind Media Private Limited
466, DDA SFS Apartments, Pocket 1, Sector 22, Dwarka,
New Delhi – 110077
books.readomania.com
email: support@readomania.com
Facebook: facebook.com/iamreadomania
Twitter: twitter.com/iamreadomania

First Published in 2017 by Readomania

ISBN: 978-93-858545-7-6

Typeset in Palatino Linotype by Shine Graphics
Printed in India by Thomson Press India Ltd.

India has traditionally been the land of storytellers and a lot of us have an inherent skill of creating good plots, good stories and good narrations. With a little encouragement and support, many more authors will be widely read and attain a place in the sun. This is the essence of *Readomania*—an initiative that nurtures emerging stars of the literary world.

It would not be an exaggeration to say that *Readomania* is the talent hunt in fiction. It goes a step beyond by not just identifying the talent but also nurturing it and showcasing it to the world. In the process, we have created a powerhouse of content.

*Readomania* has four principal interest areas—traditional print publishing, online library of short stories and poetry, literary events and products.

The print publishing works towards delivering good quality content to the readers. We publish good authors in meaningful anthologies, novels and works of narrative non-fiction. Our books stand out for their perspectives, the plots, the language and most importantly their ability to enrich lives.

Take a break, read something nice, write something beautiful. Read our books or visit us at www.readomania. com and enjoy a whole new world of literature.

'I am out with lanterns, looking for myself.'

—Emily Dickinson

*For*

*My husband, Johnny,*
*who gives me the roots to weather any storm*
*and*
*the wings to fly as high as I desire*

# About the Author

Alisha 'Priti' Kirpalani lives in Mumbai along with her husband, two daughters, one cat and over a hundred board games. Her journey with words started after she won a creative writing contest in college, an undisclosed number of decades ago. This was followed by a degree in English Literature, a short stint as a reporter and later as a copywriter.

After a career change to wife and mother, she kept the flame alive as a freelance feature writer and a secret fiction writer. She reignited her passion to be a published author when her microfiction on Twitter and her blog on *Medium* received an extremely positive response. She won the microfiction contest hosted by *Medium*'s online publication, *The Coffeelicious*. This was followed by being declared a top writer in Feminism on *Medium*.

Her e-Book of short stories, *A Smattering of Darkness—Short and Shorter Twisted Tales*, a collection of short stories encapsulating the grey shades of the human psyche, was launched in December 2015, as an experiment to introduce her writing to the reading world. It was in the top 10 of Amazon's bestsellers on release and this short anthology receives high ratings and reviews to date.

*Out With Lanterns* is the inevitable culmination of a long-cherished dream of writing a novel and the healthier alternative of comfort writing over a span of many years. Like her author name, a blend of her married and maiden names, her writing blends emotion with commiseration.

*As a woman, I play many roles simultaneously, changing colours as the need arises.*

*Through the lens of empathy, compassion and most of all understanding, I pen my stories. I believe we all face defeat, drudgery, death at some point in our lives. How do we feel? What sees us through? We are all prisoners of our minds, of the events in our lives and of those around us. The tip of the iceberg, shiny and gleaming, is not what interests me. The solid mass beneath, that which supports the brittle edifice is what fascinates me. What we frantically hide from prying eyes but what dominates each and every one of us.*

*That convoluted working of the psyche.*

ALISHA 'PRITI' KIRPALANI
Twitter: @alisha_k
Blog: https://medium.com/@alisha_k
Website: www.alishapritikirpalani.com
Email: alisha@alishapritikirpalani.com
Instagram: alisha_priti_kirpalani

# ACKNOWLEDGMENTS

This book would be incomplete, if I were not to mention the contribution of the people in my progression as a person and a writer.

My mother, Asha Thawani, who taught me every value, emphasising that of education, through her constant sacrifices.

My father, Devidas Thawani, who helps everyone that reaches out to him, beyond the call of duty and inspires my writing to touch hearts.

My daughter, Sascha Kirpalani, a brilliant psychologist and exemplary critic, who cleared my vision from the shadow of self-doubt and encouraged me to write the book I wanted.

My daughter, Tiana Kirpalani, a prolific wordsmith and exceptional reviewer, who taught me to battle against all odds, holding my hand through the barren land where this book bloomed.

My friends, Priya Sharma, Ravi and Geeta Mansukhani, for their valuable inputs and faith in my writing. Sona Sippy, for being my earliest reader many decades ago. Geeta Kewalramani, Shenaz Bhadha and Aparna Kadir for always being there.

My aunts, Tootal Motwani for cultivating the love for reading with our library jaunts and Malti Keswani, for being my first teacher and second mother.

Jaihind College and my English teachers, Mr and Mrs Shahani, Ms Rochelle D'Souza and especially Mrs Vispi Balaporia for their motivation and belief in my ability to master the language.

My mentor, friend and author par excellence, Satyarth Nayak, who gave me tireless support, asking nothing in return.

My gentlemanly publisher, Dipankar Mukherjee, my fabulous editor, Indrani Ganguly and the team at Readomania, for helping me fulfil my lifelong dream.

All my family members originating from the Thawanis, the Kirpalanis, the Ramsays and my friends, old and new, who have been a part of my cheerleading team, pushing me to write my novel, till I finally did.

The Cricket Club of India and the Library Committee for their enthusiastic efforts and invaluable patronage.

You, my reader, who gives me reason to write.

Above all, I am grateful to the Almighty for all His/Her blessings and divine protection.

Thank you.

Jai Mata Di.

ALISHA 'PRITI' KIRPALANI
December 2017

# 1

# Karin

The queue was surprisingly orderly. Perhaps, because the literary world attracted either the refined or the pretentious, who were loath to adopt the great Indian tradition of shoving and pushing. A tiny regiment of fans waited for their book to be signed by the upcoming author, Aksh Soni. He sported a five o'clock shadow of a stubble on an unremarkable yet riveting face. His thick head of hair was raven black, accentuating his smoky grey eyes. Everything else about him gave the impression of being average, be it his height, weight or complexion but he exuded a cerebral sexuality. His indisputable talent rose well above that moderate ratio and tipped the scales further in his favour. He touched his ear lobe at intervals, by force of habit. His unease was palpable as his hands twitched slightly, signing book after book. The beads of sweat on his upper lip, like an inner circle, privy to the volley of questions he answered. Aksh looked like a teenager playing the role of a studious writer in a college play.

Karin Mehra was incongruous, a definite misfit. She looked it, and felt the others around her perceived it too. Everything about her screamed 'socialite'. A chic bob with flyaway strands of impertinent silky hair, encased her unconventionally attractive face. She was taller than most of the women around her and carried her height with supreme confidence. Her chocolate-brown eyes glimmered under the black cover of eyeliner. Her strong features added to her towering persona. Karin swung her solitaire inwards, so only the gold band showed, trying futilely to synthesise into her surroundings.

She studied the crowd and realised not much had changed over the years, including the three varieties of word worms. The lowest level comprised the wordless wonders whose adoration of all things literary, raised authors to their demigod status. These were the have-nots of talent. They usually came with some aunty or nephew and chomped samosas while they mingled. Level two consisted of the word chasers. They pursued the words and situations that would light the consecrated path to publication. A word chaser was characterised by one or a combination of both constituents; khadi and/or obscure novel in hand. Lastly, the word whisperers. This species were on top of the food chain. Their faces had made it to the back cover. Their names emblazoned on the front cover. They swooshed around the place. The more lionised they were, the more vigorous their movements. The hierarchy stipulated by the quantity and quality of the entourage loitering beside them.

Even if by outward appearance it seemed otherwise, Karin belonged here. This she knew. In this world of parable, epic and fable. Away from kitty parties, academic open days and bar nights at the club. Like a neatly folded dress stowed away in a drawer, she had saved her muse and stashed it away for a time that was hers. Now was that time.

She was one person away from Aksh Soni. The enthused young girl before her screeched and gushed. Karin pictured the girl writing his name in her blood. She studied Aksh. He seemed to be courteous but it was tinged with an unmistakable air of aloofness. It was in his incisive eyes, his magnetism. They were inscrutable tunnels of gunmetal. He had the aesthetic hands of a maestro. Not the metrosexual manicured ones but hands that belonged to a classical sculpture. Abruptly the space between them was devoured and she was at the table. He smiled, extending his hand out for the book. Fumbling, she extended her hand out to him instead.

'You stole my story,' she blurted.

Aksh looked perplexed and flustered.

'Sorry?'

'This is the kind of story I would have written. Now that it is told, I do not know where to find another.' Her voice sounded strange to herself.

'My apologies, Madam,' he said, grinning. 'For a second, you had me there. May I sign our story for you?'

'Yes, please! Could you address it to K-a-r-i-n?' she mumbled.

'Karin?' he iterated.

'It is pronounced Kah-reen,' she clarified.

Her outward poise shielded her inner ruckus, as she mechanically handed him the book and watched him sign the front page. What had possessed her to blab that moronic statement? She was mortified into freeze frame. The restless, shuffling motions of people, waiting in the expanding line behind her, instigated her out of immobility. She bit her tongue to silence it into submission and chose to nod her head instead, as he handed the book back to her.

It was this setting that was unsettling. Her usual haunt of the bookstore had undergone an absolute metamorphosis to accommodate the phenomenon called Aksh Soni, as the invite flamboyantly stated. His transgression of the store was disconcerting and the place was bereft of its familiarity. All the other books had disappeared as if in some conspiracy theory, their spines had been broken and unrolled to give his novel, the red-carpet treatment. His presence had leaked into the whole space making her feel infinitesimal, her feelings of insignificance growing significantly. This was her road not taken. This is where she might have been. This could have been her. The diamond dug into her palm. A piercing reminder of the self-flagellation of this experience. Her senses reeled with an overwhelming blend of discomfiture and despondency. The hot tears scalding her almond eyes in anger, as they were held prisoner.

On the drive back home, the mantra of his signed message played in her head as she read it over and over again.

Dear Karin,

Keep seeking and your story will meet you halfway, on the horizon where imagination and inspiration become one.

Regards,

Aksh Soni

# 1A

Dear Aksh,

I am not sure if you remember me but we met at your book signing event. I was the woman who accused you of stealing my thoughts. Not exactly the most premier of introductions but hopefully it works to jog your memory. Your advice was very motivating. Thank you for your patience. I know this is the point at which I should sign off. This delicate equilibrium where I leave you with a feeling of validation about your undeniable expertise. Yet I am going to go ahead and plunge head first, gambling on the natural curiosity of a writer's mind. Will you indulge me?

Why am I writing to you? I do not know. I am going to go with the flow. My life is structured enough. Happily married for over two decades, two children and living the life. A home and office in 'the' South Mumbai. A Mercedes. Business-class excursions. And grateful for it all. But. Isn't there always a but? These mutterings in my head, like naughty children, will not rest. The missing link. The one that unifies the 'we' of matrimony to the 'I' of individuality.

Aksh, am I too old to chase a dream? Am I too weary to stand in your shoes? Mother. Wife. Daughter. Sister. Pall-bearers of my identity. Should I call it a wrap and let the story inside me, be scattered with my ashes? Will my obituary, which I intend to write in advance, be the only words my life will strew on the fields of immortality?

Drama much? Sorry.

Will I be relegated to junk mail?

Regards,

Karin

# 2

# Aksh

A nother literary festival. Another book signing. In the thick of it all, sat Aksh Soni, pimping his words in the bylanes of popularity. His whore of a novel was the belle of the ball. Everyone wanted to mount and ride on her wave of success. Fame and fortune were deferential suitors kissing his feet and all Aksh felt, was the dullness of anticlimax. His only breather was the sight of the cars scaling the Kemps Corner flyover, which was in view thanks to the full-size picture windows of the bookstore. There were two levels which were full of readers and browsers waiting to meet him. Like the cars stuck in a snarl, many people waited on the stairs, some coiled around the banister, while some sat with their butts half off the narrow width of the steps. The only difference was they did not honk furiously like the impatient drivers, expertly negotiating the carefree pedestrians who ruled the tarmac turf and hopped on and off the kerb as they pleased.

He had never imagined his writing or for that matter, his ostensibly unusual name, attracting so much scrutiny. Aksh Soni was a run-of-the-mill boy from the suburbs of Mumbai who did not want to join the LED family tradition. The LED trinity comprised lawyers, engineers, doctors. Aksh, in an act of sheer blasphemy, dumped Science and chose the professionally suicide-laden territory of English Literature. With his family's 'literature is for losers' mindset, the transpiring scenario was inevitable. Despite his father's wrath-filled disappointment and mother's tearful beseeching, Aksh did not budge on his decision. If writing was the road to starvation, then teaching would be his back-up plan.

Aksh and his father used to be kitten men once. Soft-spoken and docile. Till life transgressed and later, to worsen matters, Aksh, the good son, decided to forge his own path of poesy and passion. Thereon, like ferocious tigers, father and son regularly unleashed that torrid skirmish of words that wounded the other.

'You are going to amount to nothing, but a dime a dozen writer. Aksh, you are an idealistic fool who will realise it too late. Then you will turn into a drunken loser because failure will drive you mad, like your predecessors. I am writing your life story!'

'And when did you ever conform to the rules you are laying down for me? I am going to be a writer, Dad. With your blessings, hopefully. Without your blessings, regardless.'

Their home shook with the roars of rebellion. Then it was silent. And never quite the same again.

It was in circumstances like these, that scene seemed to crop up cunningly and nudge him into a minuscule sense of victory.

So here he was, worth more than a few dimes. All things considered, a wealthy man in the near future. A movie deal on the anvil for his first book. Considerable signing amount offers for his second book. Eligible, technically. Intelligent. And first-time lucky. At thirty-seven years of age, Aksh Soni was Lady Luck's favoured child.

Here an Aksh, there an Aksh, everywhere an Aksh, Aksh. Old McDonald marketing strategy in play for the cash cow. They had really pulled out all the stops in the bookstore to make sure of that. Ensnared in this zoo of celebrity-dom and multiple images of his own face, Aksh surveyed the cavorting line of his readers, through the invisible bars of his present-day Page-Three status. Each one like a fawning courtier, bearing gifts of appreciation. All this, in return for a few seconds of chat, a possible photo opportunity and an autograph from the reigning prince.

Specimen Number 1

The eager-beaver mother pushing her reluctant adolescent forward.

She: My child comes first in English. Do you have writing classes?

Me: No. Sorry.

Pacified with a personally signed book.

Specimen Number 2

The morose, stereotypical endeavouring writer who glares and stares, till you feel apologetic at ever being published.

He: I write occult haiku.

Me: Interesting. Where can I read your haiku?

He: On www.poetsarenotadeadsociety.com.

Mollified with a personally signed book.

Specimen Number 3

She: What does your name mean?

Me: Axis.

She: Access? Like entry?

Me: No. A-X-I-S.

Dismissed with a personally signed book.

Specimen Number 4

She: Is Aksh your real name? Means what?

Me: Axis.

She: Like the bank?

Me: Yes, like the bank.

Silenced with a personally signed book.

Specimen Number 5

She: I like your name. What does it mean?

Me: Axis.

She: Cool!

Muted with a personally signed book.

Specimen Number 6

The gushing young girl who sounds like a series of squeals, screeches and a few rushed breaths interspersed, intermittently.

She: You are the best! The best! The best! The best...

Voice peters off.

Me: Thank you.

Rewarded with a personally signed book.

Specimen Number 7

The rich chick conspicuous by her unlikely presence and whose designer sunglasses are conspicuous by their absence, save for the faint indentation on the bridge of her nose.

She: You stole my story.

Me: Eh? Phew!

Or something to that effect.

Thwarted with a personally signed book.

Well, at least she had provided the dramatic interlude.

The snake of the crowd kept shedding skin, till at long last, it slithered away and Aksh slumped in sheer relief. Behind him, in graphic contrast, a vertical poster bearing his name, a seraphic smile superimposed on his congenial face.

Aksh Soni. Named after his father Akshay Soni. The baton of paternity to be carried forward through life. The boring and vain truth behind his uncommon name.

# 2A

Hello there,

Thank you for writing in. You are definitely a lady of unpredictability, with rings on her fingers, bells on her toes and surprises up her sleeve. I am conflicted on who is more surprised by this mail. Me, who does not have the slightest inkling as to why I am writing it. Or you, who I assume, expected no response or at best, a clinical one. Usually my publicist handles this sort of thing. Well, at the risk of sounding arrogant, I do believe that fortune favours the brave. You had the courage to make an impact in that audience of adulation. So I owe you one. And no, I do not say this to every woman who accuses me of usurping her inspiration. Not that there have been that many. None, to be downright honest. I have to admit I am intrigued at a certain level with our unique encounter.

Writing is about attention grabbing ultimately. A skill, you seem to have mastered. So how do you take this bravery forward to the battlefield of books? Time has left its sweeping wounds and they have festered into constant cravings. Reach inside, bleed them out. It is as simple as that. Or as difficult as that. The rest is excess baggage. Save it for your next novel.

Sit by the ocean and visualise the words ebbing and flowing. Gather them in the palm of your hands and quench your thirst before they slip away once again.

All the best and maybe we will meet someday at a book signing, this time on the same side of the table. Stranger things have been known to happen.

Best,

Aksh

# 3

## The Gals

Secretly she called them the midwives. They had finished delivering the expected offspring, given their personal ambition step-motherly treatment, and now, after the trial by matrimonial fire, here they were, consumed by the midlife crisis. Karin studied each one of her friends. The blonde streaks distinguished members of their tribe from others. Their hair like straw, much like the poverty-bleached street urchins. The only difference, the poor did not pay five thousand rupees at the exclusive French salon.

The 'Gals Gang', as they wishfully called themselves, met for a weekly lunch date. The women took turns to choose the venue and foot the bill. The pattern and the participants remained unchanged for many years. Payal had stuck to an old faithful in her choice of cuisine. The soup, salad and sandwich buffet attracted groups of women, teenagers and business executives alike. Though the restaurant had a beautiful view of the Queen's Necklace, as Marine Drive was endearingly named, the weather was too humid to sit outdoors. Moreover, the sunlight and occasional gust of breeze was not very kind to the makeup and hair of middle-aged women. The exterior was frequented by youngsters from neighbouring colleges who had no such issues and did not care about the din of the traffic flowing through the busy Churchgate stretch either. The restaurant had started to look jaded over the span of years. Karin looked around as if she were seeing it with new eyes. It was like the place was decomposing as she was surveying it. The cracked tabletop trying to disguise its maltreatment, in vain, under the jaundiced table cloth. The cutlery and crockery had stretch marks of wear and tear, moaning under the drudgery of depletion. The dented metal name badges of the staff were indistinct. Had this happened all of a sudden or had Karin never bothered to notice? She felt a frantic rush of giddiness as she looked at her friends, like she were seeing them anew too.

There was, of course, Payal, the hostess for the day. She had obsessive compulsive disorder, and everyone except Payal knew it. A healthy heart and an even better body. It helped to trample the rogues of repetition on the treadmill. Veena was the human extractor. She siphoned out information, converted it into gossip and piously packaged it as pearls of wisdom and enlightenment to be shared with the world for its general good. Myra was the poor, little, rich girl. She had everything that money could buy except the calibre of emotional equations she hankered after, be it friend or husband. She hung around on the periphery of acceptance, hoping to enter the embrace of kinship. Nonita, or nonentity, was the filler. Her augmentation to the group was zilch but then sometimes 'no views is good news' and so she remained an introverted yet fervent participant. Sameera. If charm had a persona, it would be her. The giggly, easy-going, girly woman. Everyone instantly liked Sameera. Until...until you were perceptive enough to catch that flash of shrewdness bolting from her eyes, till it was reined in again.

By no standards were they 'gals' anymore. Not by a long shot. Years of cultivation had harvested a parasitic bonhomie, which nobody was disposed to jeopardise, including Karin. Any dissension was quickly quelled. The women were fond of each other, as much as their temperaments would allow, and the husbands became a natural extension of the gang. Sunday champagne brunches, Saturday nights at prestigious clubs and weekend getaways to Alibaug or Lonavala. Karin needed her midwives to fill her physical sphere. They were her diversion from the intensity that furtively baited her into plummeting lows. Then there were days when she wanted to suckle at that underbelly of damnation rather than be cocooned in this cardboard cut-out portrayal of life. This was one of those days.

'Hostess with the mostest, what's the topic of discussion for the day? I have a naughty one, if you need help,' offered Sameera. On Payal's behest, she looked at the women with deliberation and gleefully continued, 'The disgusting habits of our spouses. How's that for a conversation starter? I will go first because I know nobody else will venture into the twilight zone. I dare you to top Rajiv's repulsive one.' Sameera paused for effect. 'Rajiv needs to read the obituary page to relieve his constipation. The thought of corpses makes him poop. He knows every funeral taking place in town. Beat that, Veena!'

The women were agog with excitement so nobody really noticed Karin's disinterest. Veena rubbed her hands and looked around the restaurant cautiously. 'Vijay twirls the hair on his arms and legs when he is on a phone call. All matted and twisted into tiny black worms. Quite disgusting! I just ignore it but it freaks me out. Your turn, Payal.'

'Listening to Sameera and you, I don't feel that put off with Sunil. As is obvious to all and sundry, Sunil is a few strands short of certified bald. He has this annoying way of combing his hair. The few, lonely hair at the back of his head are combed all the way from one ear to another and he actually believes it does the job of camouflage. Better to go fully bald but I know it is a sore point. What is with these men and their hair? As if their virility rests in those follicles. Like that Samson chap.' Payal passed the spoon to Myra with a flourish.

'Let me think.' Myra paused then spoke breathlessly. 'Whenever Harry wakes up, he touches the tip of his tongue and applies the saliva to his face. Tip, tip, tip. He thinks it helps his acne scars. Nonita?'

'I have never really noticed anything disgusting about Sanjay. I mean, he has many disgusting habits, like the usual ones but nothing special. Karin can answer and I will try and think of something.' Nonita declined politely and they all looked towards Karin.

'Karin? A gold guinea for your thoughts, since a penny would be too passé,' enquired Sameera.

Veena chirped in, 'Yes, Karin. Even I noticed you haven't been quite here. All fine? Raoul? The girls?'

'I am fine. I don't think I slept too well last night and am feeling knackered. Sorry. Not trying to be a wet blanket.'

Sameera winked, 'Methinks Karin and Raoul struck gold last night.'

'Then Sameera, perhaps you know more about Raoul and me, than I do?'

'Tell us, tell us. Let us enjoy too, even if it is vicariously. Then we will let you off the hook.' Veena persisted excitedly.

Their laughter bristled through her senses and she wanted to deactivate their volume knobs. Karin conjured up a weak smile and mercifully the focus shifted to Payal's steroid-infused gym trainer. Lucky for her that these women were easily distracted. An outlandish thought crossed her mind. What if life was like a *MAD* comic? That segment where the shadow portrays the unexpressed truth. What was it called? The Shadow Knows. In the shadow, these women would be gargantuan mouths with tree trunk-sized duct tape on their blithering orifices.

'Karin? Are you sure you are fine?' Myra asked softly. Karin squirmed at the touch of Myra's hand on her arm. Myra's manicured fingernails with their black polish, were a replica of a vulture's claws, digging into her wrist. A very shaky vulture. 'Karin?'

'Sorry, Myra. One of those days. My body clock is so messed up lately.' Karin replied in a measured tone.

Myra lowered her voice. 'I have some tablets, to de-stress your mind. You will sleep better, too. If you want... They have really helped me loosen up.'

Karin shook her head in a tactful refusal, thinking, 'they really do not seem to have helped you', as she gingerly patted Myra's sweaty palms.

Karin felt a stab of self-reproach and mortification at the viciousness of her feelings. Everything was an action replay and the effort to partake was draining her. This stream of consciousness had been uncoiling in her head since the book signing and had worsened matters. Whether it was Raoul, the girls and now her friends, they seemed like hurdles that she had to overcome, to touch base with herself. It had to stop! She excused herself and decided to call Raoul. An out-of-the-blue call with nil practicality. Or an erotic message? Her head was aching with the exertion of decision making. What was wrong with her?

Then she saw it. Through the maze of the inbox on her smart phone, there it was. Sandwiched between *'Navneet Constructions announces its mega township enterprise in Bhandup'* and *'Urgent message for "Mr" Karin Mehra. You have won GBP 100,000'* lay languorously, *'From Aksh Soni.'*

She clutched her phone, letting the mail lie unopened, tantalisingly impregnated with potential. Bracing herself for disappointment and yet filled with an intoxicating rush, she let the moment savour her being. A deep breath later, the words emerged shyly, almost as if they knew how long she had secretly coveted them.

# 3A

Oh my God! Thank you! You wrote back!
  Suspended in disbelief,

Karin

# 3B

Dear Aksh,

Sorry about that crazed outburst. At times, I have a lack of impulse control, as is apparent. I was so taken aback at receiving a response from you, that my fingers were triggered into spontaneous combustion. Once more, thank you.

In a delusional assumption, I dare to hope that it was the lure of my words that drew yours into this cyber waltz of correspondence. Was I special enough to merit a personal reply? If I hazard a guess, you seem to be the sort of person who has been shoved into a gigantic pothole of public relations, when all you would rather do is sit by the meadows and ruminate alongside the cows.

After that awkward analogy, I should retreat into oblivion but this blank page holds such beguiling promise. A neon light that flares 'Carpe Diem!'

So here I go again, trying to seize the day.

At this juncture, as I write to you, I feel alive in a way that I have not felt in forever. Let me explain, before you dismiss me as a cougar trying to fill my empty space with a new toy-boy. Yes, I am forthright so you do not misconstrue my intent. I have a co-actor for all my roles— maternal, filial and spousal. It is my impassioned, artistic alter ego that has no place to call home. I am in quest of a creative coalition with a mentor and a motivator. Someone that will help give birth to my tale and will witness this labour of love, by my side. I want you to be that someone, Aksh. My chosen one.

At the risk of making it sound like a pencil brand, will you be my write-mate?

I want or offer nothing more or nothing less.

Simply that cascading river of words, that will keep soul and sanity afloat.

Why me?

Try me.

Warm regards,

Twice-Lucky Karin?

# 4

# Aksh and Sia

A ksh watched Sia sleep. The gargoyle-shaped silhouettes cast by the bedside lamp, staked claim on different parts of her body. The silhouette on the cheek looked, well, almost cheeky, as it crouched possessively. Aksh shifted the lamp marginally and it was like the gargoyles panicked and changed shape in a bid to remain indistinguishable. He did this a few times. It was like watching others touch Sia. An intimacy which he was sharing voluntarily and voyeuristically. The prospect excited him. Then it sickened him.

If he had to describe Sia in one word, it would be pretty. She was petite, reminding him of a pixie. Sia and he had been together for six years. Long before he was *the* Aksh Soni. His recent prosperity had empowered Aksh enough to ask her to move in with him. Much to the chagrin of both sets of parents, she did. The house was a one-bedroom apartment in the heart of South Mumbai. Though it was on the other side of the tracks, in Charni Road, he was one railroad crossing away from the coveted sea. He had spent most of his life, moving from post to post, as his father's army transfers dictated. After his father's early retirement, they settled in Chembur. The Chembur of then was perceived as a gas tank because of the pollution levels in the vicinity. Aksh spent his college years studying in St Xavier's College on the other side of town, switching streams from Science to Humanities like a quick change artist. The British history of Mumbai was preserved in South Mumbai, in its architecture as much as its snobbery. He was drawn to befriend the smartly dressed girls and boys from town side who exuded confidence but they seemed almost godlike in their inaccessibility. He used to love walking the melodiously named streets, Ash Lane, Ropewalk Street of Kala Ghoda. The Jehangir Art Gallery and the Asiatic Library were to Aksh a treasure trove of culture. Colaba, Marine Drive, Chowpatty were places where the sea matched the fathoms of a young Aksh's thoughts. In those five years, Aksh's resolve was to live here, in South Mumbai, someday and that resolution had finally come true. One day, in the not-so-distant future, he was determined to belong to that exclusive club of those who wore their wealth and westernisation, like a second skin, if not by birthright, then by outright purchase of property. For now, this dingy apartment was all he could afford, but he felt a welcoming to the beginning of his dreams. In this congested, commercial city, every square inch of living space was an exorbitance and the lease had eaten up most of his freshly earned gains but it was worth the price, despite the below average condition of the house. Aksh suspected the mattress had bed bugs, a childhood phobia, but the wily critters seemed omnipresent even in their invisibility. The landlord had painted the walls an awful blue colour, in a botched attempt to create a soothing ambience. The leakage-infested ceiling had paint peeling like stalactites. It was not much but it was his home, his first ever home. Strangely, ever since Sia and he shared the same roof, sleep seemed to be eluding him. Insomnia was his staunch companion, hanging around like a jealous lover. Aksh often spent these nights conceptualising Sia and their milieu.

As he looked at Sia, he tried to find an answer to her continual question. And he still did not know the answer. In their early years together, she would invariably query him. 'Do you love me, Aksh? Do you see a future for us? I need to know.'

'Sia, let me put it this way, if I were to marry, it would be you. Love? Why else would I be here? I am not a man to pigeonhole feelings. What's the rush anyway?'

She loved him enough to subsist on the measly morsels he tossed her way. Aksh felt villainous now and again, especially when he could perceivably feel her emotions looming over his reticence. Her avowals of love were met with a kiss or a grunt. Sia understood his idiosyncrasies or at the very least she put up with him. He hurt her frequently with his restraint but she understood and accepted it. He did not leave her with much choice in the matter.

There was that one time, three years ago, when she actually left him. In retrospect, it was the last time she mentioned a future together. Aksh had started working on his novel, so many a meal revolved around its development. He had a suspicion that she used to listen to his monologues with unabated interest because she was insecure that he would isolate her in his dedication to the endeavour. She snatched the interval of silence, forced by his eating, and filled the speed bump in the conversation with her lack of certainty about their future.

'Aksh, where are we headed? Are we ever going to marry, have kids? Live happily ever after? I know romance is not your genre,' she jeered lightly but her eyes were humourless.

'Sia, marriage is not an impossibility but an improbability. Not only with you, with anyone. I do not mean to hurt you but the yoke of marriage seems too stifling. I am the square peg that you are trying to put through the round hole of wedlock. I cannot ensure the future and I do not want to lead you down the garden path. This, the way we are, it works for me. Take me as I am, here and now. It is the pinnacle of me. One time offer only!' Aksh tried to jest away her deep-rooted fears about their relationship.

Sia picked up her handbag and with utter steely detachment declared she was done and dusted with him.

Aksh let her go without a murmur. He never called. He just wrote and rewrote chapter after chapter of his novel.

She came back a few weeks later, unannounced, unexpected.

It was like she had never left. Thereafter, she reconciled to the fact that she was boxed in that inflexible position of being back to square one.

They never spoke of that day or of marriage to date. Despite her weakness for him, Sia had too much pride to bring it up again. Sia believed she knew Aksh better than he knew himself. He would find his way to her someday but she was not going to lose her dignity while he stumbled through his own obstacle of emotional impotence to get there. The time apart taught her one thing—she could live without him but she could not live with begging him for a commitment and degrading herself. Getting him to marry her was not the be-all and end-all of her existence. If she left the domestic bliss bit at the doorstep, he was everything she wanted in a man—intelligent, liberal, humorous, caring, and a good lover. She was resilient and independent enough to enjoy the present with Aksh without worrying about a future with him.

As she lay noiselessly asleep beside him, he speculated about what would have happened if she had not come back. Sia turned around as Aksh's phone flashed. It was like lightning had struck the walls of the room. She squinted enquiringly at him and then went back to sleep. Aksh half smiled in apology and rubbed her shoulder reassuringly. Her body went back into a steady rhythm of breathing.

The phone flashed again. Aksh grappled with it and recognised the email address of the sender. A twinge of irritation passed through him. Why was this Karin woman stalking him? And at this hour too! He should never have responded to her mail. Bloody mistake! He had not admitted it to himself initially, but his middle-class, suburban self had been flattered that a downtown born and bred, upper-crust woman admired his work. It was like gourmet icing on the cake of his fan base but he had not anticipated her persistence. She wrote, he replied, she thanked him. End of story. Now what did she want?

As he read Karin's words, they engulfed Aksh, a primal scream resonating with the savagery of unfulfilled desire. The impactful force of her mail caught him completely unaware. The stark purity of her yearning to write, reminded him of a time lost and gone, leaving in its wake, this sledgehammer reminiscence. A time when nothing was planned by publicists and publishers. He sorely missed that utopia. If he was being honest with himself, there was a tad bit of gloating too. She was one of those women out of his league that he could never muster up courage to approach, and today, he, the boy from Chembur, was the one being pursued with a mission. In an uncharacteristically impulsive move, Aksh changed course. He typed two words, hesitated, typed a bit more, and then punched the send key.

# 4A

Karin,

Why not? Your not-so-indecent proposal might be a-musing.

Aksh

# 4B

Aksh,
Are you serious? Really?

Karin

# 4C

Karin,

Though I would like to understand the job description before I unofficially accept your offer.

Aksh

# 4D

Aksh,

If you were the 9-to-5 type of person, I would certainly go into the gory details, but you are way beyond and above that. This once, desert your acclaimed words and lead me through the wilderness, till I find my own voice.

Karin

# 4E

Karin,

Shazam! Done! Ye convincing one!

Aksh

# 5

## Karin and Raoul

'Karin, if you don't want to watch it, just say so. You have made me wait, twiddling my thumbs, since half an hour. What are you so busy doing?' Raoul sounded miffed as he walked into the study.

'Just give me ten minutes, Raoul. I have to dash off some emails. And stop snapping at me! Go flip through some channels till I am done!' Karin said brusquely.

'Thank you for the permission to channel surf. I could have finished an episode of *The Mentalist* while waiting for you idly, but when it...' Raoul's voice droned and Karin put on some music to blast it into atoms of silence. Raoul threw up his hands in resignation and charged off into the bedroom.

Their colossal Cuffe Parade house seemed deceptively small as their voices boomeranged through the walls. Karin wondered if the maids could hear them in the kitchen. The help was an encroachment yet they were the pillars that supported the framework of their privileged lifestyles. It perturbed Karin that she might be the gateway drug of gossip in the menial grapevine. The prestigious building had a health club, recreation room along with other amenities and its crowning glory was an uninhibited view of the Arabian Sea. Cuffe Parade, a locality, reclaimed from the sea, which now lay in deference at its feet, was at the southernmost tip of Mumbai. It was a quiet, cosmopolitan area except when the rich kids of the neighbouring school were heading home, creating daily traffic jams which had the elite residents in an activist uproar. The sea-facing study was Karin's cocoon and her temple of thought, a fact attested and accessorised by the decor of the area. It was peppered with her books, the computer and a top-of-the-line recliner. Her prized Venetian masks adorned the burgundy accent wall. Her treasury of Fabergé eggs in the Victorian cabinet was enviable. She loved the intricacy of their lacquer work. Each curve, each gradation, so industriously detailed on their oval facets.

In the serenity of her study, she realised her reaction was erratic and unjustified. Between Raoul's love for crime shows and her interest in sitcoms, the twain only met in a nightly custom of watching a mutually acceptable show. Karin downloaded pilot episodes and once a show piqued their interest, it became the comforter under which they lay in companionable proximity. Raoul had been shooting blanks at her and she had been dodging the bullet of television, all evening.

Mundanity is a marriage's arch nemesis. Karin and Raoul were friends before they were lovers. This helped to fill in the blanks that truant passion so often leaves behind. The gaping holes had been plugged with carefully cultivated allied interests. Karin was astute and had realised long ago, that sex, love and beauty are available freely in the marketplace of relationships. Need—a feeling of incompletion without the partner—that was the ploy, if the ultimate target was an enduring marriage. The symbiotic intercourse of dependence.

Karin knew she was bending their unspoken marital rules but her ennui was all pervasive and she wanted to wallow in it. She thirsted for an imaginary enclosure which nobody could infiltrate except her harlot thoughts wanting to spread themselves on a blank sheet of paper. The demanding schedule of running home and hearth, punctured her sanctum so relentlessly that she was left gasping for the air of reclusion.

Karin needed time out. That's all. Why was she not telling Raoul about Aksh? Or about this arsenic-soaked fervour to write which had been poisoning her mind lately? Between her hormones and her head, the imbalance was creating havoc.

She walked into the bedroom. The television was doing the dance of decibel levels as Raoul switched from channel to channel. He glanced at her, gave her the cold shoulder and intently watched the teleshopping network hard-selling a magnetic bracelet on the contention that it would radically change the well-being of its wearer.

This was a vintage Raoul characteristic. He expressed emotion by acting overly unemotional. He looked forward to their inviolable routine and Karin's disinterest was fazing him but he would never admit it, even to himself.

'Sorry, Raoul. I am coming down with something, I think. I have been feeling lightheaded and out of sync. I have a migraine, too. Why don't you watch something else? I will rest it out in the other room. Sorry, baby.'

'Take a tablet or something. You can stay here. I will watch the news on mute. I am quite sleepy.' He tapped the bed. Karin lay down and Raoul played with her hair gently. It felt like an intrusion and she was ashamed of her antipathy. She felt like apologising for the complexity of her persona. He was considerably more transparent. She felt like she had brought him to the edge of seemingly still waters and he could not see the churning of the predatory undercurrents which were always lapping at their feet.

She heard light snoring and saw Raoul had dozed off, upright. She switched off the lights, covered him with a duvet and repentantly ran her hand gently across his hair. He moved slightly and then cosied into slumber.

In the darkness, she felt a contrite but uplifting rush of freedom. Her contemplation pranced around untethered and made its way to Aksh Soni. She read his mails yet another time. Until this point, she had jumped into the fray, impulsively, whether it was their first meeting or writing to him. She had nothing to lose. She had no expectation of gain. But now she was on this balancing beam, worrying continuously about her next step. Any floundering or faltering would send her crashing down again, back to rock bottom.

She dreamed that night, of being on a swing, in the middle of nowhere. Large phantom hands kept pushing the swing roughly and as hard as she tried, she could not get off. Suddenly, she was tossed midair and found herself falling off a cliff and then miraculously she was holding on to a lifeline made of paper. As she tried clinging on, the train of paper kept ripping. The falling fragments of blue ink blended with the blue sea, which foamed agitatedly beneath her flailing legs.

# 5A

*'I look at you and see all the ways a soul can bruise and I wish
I could sink my hands into your flesh and light lanterns across
your spine so you know that there's nothing but light when
I see you.*

*The loneliest people are the kindest. The saddest people
smile the brightest. The most damaged people are the wisest.
All because they do not wish to see anyone else suffer the way
they do.'*

No, that was not written by me. Though I wish it was
and if only I could write with that degree of potency.
Instead, crawling out of my mind, come these squashed
slugs of stories, the slimy remnants of worthlessness. So
have you ever read Shinji Moon's *The Anatomy of Being*?
You have something in common with Shinji. I wanted to
be her. I want to be you. I want to spit fiery ingenuity,
till all around me is aglow.

Shinji wrote these lines in her late teens. You are
obviously younger than I am. I have done nothing much
comparatively. Yes, wife, mother and the whole nine yards
that go with it. It is almost like once I took my husband's
name, I sold my soul to the matrimonial devil. I am but
the sum total of all my duties. In the dregs of all this
duty, I need to find my dismembered debris. They are
somewhere, my stone-cold bones of self.

Can I tell you the truth? I write this and I feel I am read.
It seems enough. For now. You, who rides the vessel of
victory, thank you for not trampling on my dreams. My
heart is in my mouth but I need to ask this, Aksh. This

self-detonating grenade of a question. Why are you even bothering with me?

I think I have had an angst relapse. Are the puberty years a preparatory state to the midlife crisis? Is this even the fabled midlife crisis? Am I rambling? I guess it is because I am on tenterhooks. Now that the dam is overflowing, I do not know which part will spill over and reach out to you. Or perhaps wash you away. Do I let you into my real world, the backdrop to every tale I hope to tell? Or do I confine myself to displaying the wares of my stories and wait till you help me choose the one that sells itself?

Your wish is my command, Mentor.

Waiting and awaiting,

Karin

# 5B

Dear Karin,

I give you Matsuo Basho, in barter for Shinji Moon.

*'In this poor body, composed of one hundred bones and nine openings, is something called spirit, a flimsy curtain swept this way and that by the slightest breeze. It is spirit, such as it is, which led me to poetry, at first little more than a pastime, then the full business of my life. There have been times when my spirit, so dejected, almost gave up the quest, other times when it was proud, triumphant. So it has been from the very start, never finding peace with itself, always doubting the worth of what it makes.'*

*Basho*

*(Translated by Lucien Stryk)*

My strength, according to widespread opinion, lies in writing about men but writing to me is as graceful, as feminine, as enigmatic, as powerful, as the Mother Goddess herself.

I worship her, this sinuous art, revere her in every form.

As should you.

*The abacus boasts, 'The world counts on me.'*

*The alphabet gently whispered, 'Preachings, psalms, prayers count on me.'*

Is there a fitting time to pray?

You have found your calling. You have found your faith. Now practice it.

'*The marching legions of women going about their allegiance, through the minefields of emotion. The commanders in this concentration camp of marriage, use their manhood and money to keep the women in formation. Terrorised by the notion of ageing alone, without the title of a "Mrs" through life, they robotically march on. Their chests satiated with maternal needs, heave in their armour plates of glittering diamonds and gold. Sometimes they look at each other and smile in commiseration at the suppressed longings in their hearts. To belong to someone. At the minimum, that mission has been accomplished. The flaming red of the traditional bindi, glaring like a swastika, silences all the babel in their heads. Left, right, inhale, exhale. She, the errant wife, slips into line, at last, behind her man. Left, right, left, right, left....*'

An Aksh Soni original.

Break free, albeit for a while, Karin.

Write and the paper will sigh and expose its black ash curls, as it is set aflame. The words will stand naked, begging for the torch of your arson. The pen will quaver ecstatically waiting to penetrate the chaste whiteness of each page, spasmodically. *La petite mort*, rewritten and redefined.

*Ecrire, ma chere.*

Aksh

# 6

## The *Jugalbandi*

Dear Aksh,

Thank you for bringing Basho to me. Thank you for that impeccable parallelism.

In return, I bring myself to you.

Did I disclose I am a proficient list maker? Do not laugh. It is an art form in itself.

Nomenclature: Karin Mehra

Chronological statistics: Depends on how I am feeling on the given day. Not over the hill but close enough. Forty-six, fine?

Me in three: Sensitive, lively, artistic.

Incessant interests: Reading, writing, writing, writing. Throw in some dancing.

Colour choices: Aqua blue and violet.

City of dreams: Barcelona.

Persistent phobias: Cockroaches, maggots, and being buried alive.

Pet peeves: Chipped nail varnish, unkempt hands and feet, diabetes-inducing vocal cords.

Music mojo: Il Divo, Mozart, Poets of The Fall, Gregorian, Foreigner. A mixed bag of melody.

Bathroom beat: When I am blue, it is 'Broken Wings' by Mister Mister. When I am planning to paint the town red, it is 'Mamma Mia' by Abba.

Movie masterpieces: *Blue Jasmine, All About my Mother, Life is Beautiful, Black Swan.*

Bedazzling books: *The Ancestral Skeleton* by Aksh Soni, *The Bell Jar* by Sylvia Plath, *Silk* by Alessandro Baricco, *The Kite Runner* by Khaled Hosseini, *The Time Keeper* by Mitch Albom.

Admired entity: Gautama Buddha.

Words worth: Iridescent, mellifluous.

Quotable quotient: 'And still, after all this time,

The sun never says to the Earth,

"You owe me."

Look what happens with

A love like that,

It lights the whole sky.'

—Hafiz

True confession: I wanted to be a belly dancer.

Are you up for the Karin List Challenge?

Karin

# 6A

Dear Shakira,

I am up for a challenge at all times except if it involves belly dancing or any form of dancing.

Nomenclature: Aksh Soni.

Chronological statistics: Thirty-seven.

Me in three: Reserved, creative, cynical.

Incessant interests: Writing, writing, writing and then some more writing. The internet's lesser known poets. Photography, since some things are arresting only in clear-cut reality.

Colour choices: Black. White. Matches my choice in people too.

City of dreams: Ladakh. The world is an oyster that I still have to crack open.

Persistent phobias: Writer's block. My agent's phone calls.

Pet peeves: Most of my relatives. Soap operas. Sappy novels.

Music mojo: Kitaro, Hans Zimmer, Yanni, Kenny G. The vocals detract from the music and my experience of it, so I am partial to instrumental tracks.

Bathroom beat: As previously elucidated, I know no lyrics so I hum 'Speak Softly Love' from *The Godfather* or something that sounds like it. 'Chariots of Fire' by Vangelis is my melody to beat the mournful.

Movie masterpieces: *The Godfather, Inception, My Left Foot.*

Bedazzling books: *The Old Man and the Sea* by Ernest Hemingway, *The Sherlock Holmes* series by Sir Arthur Conan Doyle, all works by Tony Parsons and Haruki Murakami and definitely *The Kite Runner* by Khaled Hosseini.

Admired entity: Abraham Lincoln.

Words worth: Elixir, serendipity.

Quotable quotient: 'And those who were seen dancing were thought to be insane by those who could not hear the music.'

—Friedrich Nietzsche

True confession: I watch Tom and Jerry cartoons to unwind.

I truly have to confess I have no idea why I am completing this infantile challenge.

Aksh

# 6B

Dear Aksh,

I already feel I know more about you than what is broadcasted in your *Wikipedia* page. Kudos for giving in to my infantile challenge. Life without my lists would be listless!

Tell me, do you remember how you started writing? Mine started with a list. No jokes. I was in school and making a timetable for my exams. Before I knew it, I was writing a poem rather than studying. I never did stick to that timetable but from that time onwards, I would scribble unfailingly. Fight with my friends. Write. Quarrel with my parents. Write. Happy. Write. Sad. Write. My fountain pen felt like a wizard's wand that transformed my feelings into sparkling poems.

That heady feeling, that satisfying aftermath, is what I want to recapture and temper with the seasoning of experience and exposure.

I want to dish out a book that has been worth the wait.

A book that satiates.

Before it gets too late.

Karin

# 6C

Dear Karin,

The rains depressed me. They still do. Those dreary droplets were a dampener and kept me housebound when all I wanted to do was run. Running was my escapism. I never partook in any school race because running to me was a sacred rite that brought stability to any turbulence or triumph. A private passion.

*Listening to the pitter patter of my padlock as it poured.*

That was the first line I ever wrote.

So the malevolent monsoon paradoxically set the mood for the madness, that was writing.

As innocence went into the incinerator, maturity brought forth frenzied stories. You could say my mind went into a 'talespin' and struck the only direction it had ever found.

A single-minded undertaking coupled with a dollop of skill and sprinkled with some luck.

Fortunately, it was not a recipe for disaster.

Aksh Soni *à la mode*

# 7

# Sia and the Swinging Singles

'Come on Aksh! How can this be an issue always? It's an annual office brunch, not a weekly one! Can you please get dressed? Please?' Sia was exasperated but kept her anger in check. She knew that losing her cool would give Aksh the exit he so desired.

'I tag along every year like Sia's little lamb, don't I? Give me a break. Two social outings in a single day is an exercise in eternal torture. I can't miss the damn wedding so I'm going to have to give this brunch a pass. You know I so hate to miss it, as much as I love the inane inside jokes and the same faces which seem to be stuck like a scratched DVD, over the last six years,' he added cheekily. Aksh had made up his mind and Sia knew it was going to be impossible to convince him otherwise.

He stretched out on the bed, knowing he was off the hook. At times like these, she wondered what was it about him that made her accept his annoying and often hurtful peculiarities. Was their relationship like that joke? What did the masochist say to the sadist? Hit me. Hit me. And the sadist replied: No. I won't. No. I won't.

What was there about this man that she could not seem to let go? Was she just one of those women who loved the challenge of a difficult man? As she bent over to wear her shoes, Aksh jumped off the bed in front of her. He had switched on Gloria Gaynor's 'I Will Survive' and in a ridiculously exaggerated hip swing, lip synced the song, yelling, 'I won't survive. I won't survive.' Sia wanted to tear her hair out but she felt her heart melting. She loved him. His brooding, his madness, his passion, all of him.

She shook her head and sighed, 'Fine! Stay home but you better make it up to me in the evening. I do not want to deal with your zillion relatives on my own while you look for the nearest escape route. By the way, I am glad you took up writing as a career instead of singing. Wise move.'

'Ouch! All is forgiven. Come home, Sia.' Aksh the joker, made a guest appearance on demand and he inevitably managed to worm his way out of a sticky situation. 'Look at the bright side, you will be single and ready to mingle with your ardent fan, who I guarantee, will be delighted to know that I will not be gracing the occasion. I consider it to be my good deed for the day, giving Vinay from Marketing, a chance to market himself. Have fun!'

It bugged her. His complete lack of jealousy towards any male attention she received. On the contrary, the interest shown by other men amused him. Sia would have hated a jealous man but Aksh was the other extreme and his indifference bothered her. She picked up her handbag before the muddle in her head rose again. 'See you in a bit and please start getting ready. Your mother has asked me to make sure we get there on time.' Aksh flopped back on the bed and covered his head with a pillow, stifling a groan.

She reached late. The theme for this year was 'Burgers, Beers and Bowling'. Entering from the bright sun outside, the neon-lit darkness of the bowling alley looked like a scene from *Moulin Rouge*. The tall tables were littered with beer bottles, French fries and half-eaten burgers.

Roars of enthusiastic cheering intermingled with even more enthusiastic cursing as the competing teams fought for victory. A few hands waved out at her as she waved back. Vinay Apte walked towards her with a questioning look on his face.

'Aksh not coming? You both are on our team,' asked Vinay. Sia shook her head in reply. 'Then I guess with our combined bowling skills and one man less, we better get set for last place,' joked Vinay.

'Vinay from Marketing' was what most women would describe as a decent and dependable guy. As Sia watched him bowl, she wondered if he actually did like her. Aksh seemed to think so, or was he just pulling her leg? Come to think of it, Vinay was single, and to her best knowledge had never shown interest in any woman or for that matter, man, in the office. As his ball rolled into the gutter, he looked towards her with an apologetic look.

'Your turn. Save us from a complete disaster.' He said as he touched her hand inadvertently and then pulled it away awkwardly. Sia was terrible at bowling. The ball landed with a thud and made its way to the gutter without much ado.

'Well, that's at least one thing we have in common, Sia. We suck at bowling.' Sia laughed and told the other three team members, 'Sorry guys! The ball is in your court, or should I say...gutter?'

They sat down on the hard metal chairs, waiting for their turn and watched the game in a self-conscious silence. Vinay broke the ice. 'So how come alone? Aksh is out of town?'

'He wasn't feeling up to it. We have to attend his cousin's wedding in the evening so he gave this a miss. He would have probably joined us in a hat-trick of gutter balls.' Sia said with a lightness she did not feel. Despite the presence of the surrounding racket, there was a tricky silence between them.

'Lucky for us that you came, regardless. I mean, I am happy you came....I mean...you know it is good that you decided to come....' Vinay was stumbling on his words.

'I am going to be leaving now. We have to get to the wedding early. I just dropped in to show off my bowling skills.' Sia said her good-byes ignoring Vinay's obviously disappointed face. Aksh was right. Vinay did seem to have a soft spot for her. The faster she got out of here, the better it was for both of them. Usually, they did not have opportunities for a one-on-one interaction. Was Vinay her type? He seemed relaxed and uncomplicated, that they definitely had in common. He would make a good boyfriend or husband, though not for her. Peculiarly, his type was not her type. Why? Dull. That's what she found most men, including Vinay, when compared to the enigma of Aksh. It dawned on her that after so many years together, she understood Aksh despite all his complexities and as much as she hated his emotional detachment and what it did to her, she felt special that he had chosen her to be by his side. That's where she wanted to be that very moment, at home, right beside him. Other men could offer her their hearts and their selves on a platter but the problem was she only wanted that from Aksh. Reality hit Sia hard there and then. Even if Aksh could not love her as passionately as the characters he created in his stories, for Sia, he was the love of her life.

# 8

# The Wedding

Aksh had evolved into a bastard. By his own declaration. An ongoing occurrence and absurdly it was accentuated the most, when it came to his parents. It was like they had given birth to a good, dependable son, who had been switched long after birth, to this self-centred, insensitive variant. Frankly, if Sia had not coerced him into giving his elderly parents time, he would have lived life like the stork had brought him into this world.

His mother had called thrice since the morning and he let the phone ring on, testing her tenacity. She never gave up. She accepted it as the price one pays for having an eminent son. Today she had outdone herself in resoluteness and with Sia away at brunch, Aksh conceded defeat.

'Yes, Mom. No, Mom. Okay, Mom.' Patience, patience, patience.

It was Aksh's cousin's wedding. Giving in to his mother's entreaties, Aksh had helped out his uncle with the financial liability of the wedding, contributing a small but helpful sum. Money was a ramification of fame that Aksh had put to good use. Not that it was pouring in but it was a mammoth step up from the frugal life he had lived so far. The wedding was close to the airport, at the other end of town. Sia had coordinated fetching Aksh's parents. When he saw them walk towards the car, his heart constricted with involuntary tenderness.

They seemed to be older each time he met them, which was not that often. Sia and he got out to assist them get into the low-slung, second-hand Honda car. Reena Soni always seemed to dawdle behind her husband. For a slim woman, she had the sluggish movements of a far heavier one. Despite years of wearing sarees, she still seemed to drape them inexpertly. From her conservative hairstyle to her antiquated glasses, Reena looked exactly like the homely woman she was.

Akshay Soni had a full head of white hair, shimmering silver in the amber sunlight. He seemed taller than he was, because of his erect carriage. His grey eyes were a dead giveaway to Aksh's parentage. Aksh unfurled his disinclined fingers as they sought to make contact with his father's coarse, thick hands. His father shrugged off Aksh's helping hand and let his arthritic, wobbling leg bear the brunt of his dignity. Irritation dashed through Aksh. The stubbornness of his father was hammering the wedge tautly in place, right between them. Sia and his mother tried their level best to displace the edginess in the car with their twittering.

'They want to make my book into a film, Dad.' Aksh almost bit his tongue after he ran off at the mouth.

'Good.'

'That's it, Dad? Good? Well, thank you, I suppose.' This is what frustrated Aksh the most. Why does a middle-aged, self-sufficient man still need the ratification of his father? How does the knife of paternity have the power to cut so unkindly and then dig even deeper into the gut? Each and every single, lousy time!

'You know, Uncle, there are talks of Amitabh Bachchan playing the role of the judge. Can you imagine your favourite actor in a character created by your son? I feel Aksh modelled the character on you.' Sia's frenetic attempt to salvage the situation irked Aksh. She sounded imbecilic in her pandering. Why was she sucking up to his father anyway? His father was hardly the scenic route to fast-track nuptials, if that was her intention.

Mom caught the ball in a smooth pass. 'All my friends are so excited by the idea of seeing little Aksh the bookworm, becoming a superstar celebrity. Everyday, some friend or the other calls to tell me that Aksh was in so and so newspaper. Akshay, you remember that photo where I felt Aksh looked exactly like you? Where was it? The *Bombay Times* party? Akshay?'

'I don't remember, Reena.' With that statement, Akshay Soni determinedly blocked the goal and the ball was thrown right out of the field. Nobody was interested in playing the game anymore. The car ride was relatively uneventful after that.

The wedding hall had a melange of guests when they entered. The decor was markedly gaudy in patches and understatedly elegant in parts. Too many cooks had definitely created this mishmash broth. Peacock feathers and marigolds on the stage outshining the newlyweds. White linen and faux pearls on the tables. The contradictory disarray unsettled Aksh for some reason. Or as usual it was the family gatherings that made him ill at ease. That feeling was the most consistent component in the disparate environment.

Aksh noticed that his relatives did not backslap him nowadays but viewed him with something akin to reverence. Most of them. A few passed snide asides and went out of their way to look unaffected by his attendance. They would wait for him to make the first move at acknowledgement. Except for Aunt Pammi. Her mannerisms were as constant as the Pole Star. She pulled at Aksh's cheeks, as always, smacking them with her thick lipstick-ravaged lips. No retreat, no surrender from the invasion of Aunt Ruby's robust lack of moderation, as Aksh lay swathed in her folds of perspiration-drenched layers of fat. The other members of the dysfunctional dynasty were excessively complicated and competitive. Nothing much had changed over the years. Remoteness was the safety net Aksh had acquired when he was submerged in this sea of sharks. The annoyance persisted and Aksh remembered the line from a film he had seen and been dying to use. 'Excuse me, you are mistaking me for someone who cares.' Aksh knew it was prudent to play the reverential son, nephew, cousin, uncle. It was less tedious than dealing with the guilt trip from his mom and Sia. These rites of passage were innumerable but then what cannot be cured must be endured.

Sia's rampant curls were glistening with glitter as she strutted around the hall, mingling with his family. She played with her hair, a traitorous divulgence to Aksh, about her internal tenseness. Whatsoever, she relished these outings where she felt a sense of belonging. The family welcomed her with beatific smiles even if at the outset, their live-in status was a subject of much scandal and speculation. What is it about most Indian women, even progressive ones like Sia, that they will bend over backwards for the stamp of approval from their boyfriend or husband's family? Aksh mulled over this standing at the bar. He dissected her into nanoscopic segments of examination from afar.

Sia was small and fragile like her name. Her hair was what attracted Aksh to her, when he saw her at an intercollegiate festival for the first time. It was an unruly, glorious mane perched on her dainty face, in a becoming antithesis. Small mercies that she had not fallen prey to the straightening iron or that cysteine crap. Those briers of locks were so goddamn unsightly. It would take an axe to comb them. They lost touch, then met again at the advertising agency where Sia, who was four years his junior, joined as a graphic designer and Aksh worked as a copywriter. From late-night brainstorming sessions to midnight coffee, it was escalating advancement into a relationship. What was it now? Six years? Did he love her? He said it to her after she said it to him. I love you too. What did it mean anyway? It was too much of a disruption to go down that road of uncertainty. The ride was rough at times but for most parts it was smooth and he had no interest in complicating life further. Sia's family lived in Delhi and though they did not like the state of affairs, they had no choice but to lump it. He was a fine catch. Just a bit slippery. Lately, they welcomed Aksh warmly on the rare instances they met, but he could still sense their vexation at his reluctance to make an honest woman out of Sia.

Aksh glanced at the mirror behind the bartender. The suit and tie looked like they were throttling him. Still another Sia and mother salvo of insistence. Fish in a suit. He made a fish-like movement with his lips. You will never reel me in.

'Would you like another wine, Sir?' asked the bartender who thought Aksh had asked for a refill. Aksh had recently cultivated a taste for wine. Besides being a drink that could be held for an extended period over long-drawn conversations that he was inevitably dragged into, the stem of the wine glass served as a distraction for his twitchy fingers.

'Sure. Why not?' Aksh smiled, as he waved to another distant cousin and prayed the guy would stay distant and not walk up for a round of insipid chat.

'Hi there. Mom wants us to go on stage to wish Ajay and Seema.' Sia tucked her arm in his and lead him away.

'Yes, Commander!' said Aksh and broke out into a march-like gait.

'I can see someone is in a wicked mood. Keep it going till we reach home,' Sia grinned at him.

'If I pull through this night, I will be your prisoner, captivating maiden. You can take my body hostage,' teased Aksh.

Sia was still red in the face when they reached the queue waiting to meet the newlyweds. They sidled into line near his parents. Gift given. Photo taken. They looked like any normal, happy family. The camera does lie. Not a sentence had dared to break the impasse between Aksh and Akshay Soni all night.

'Thank you for taking some of the strain off your uncle, Aksh.' Reena said, as she clenched her son's arm in gratitude. 'Please, for my sake, sort it out with your father. You know he loves you. Please.'

'It's only money, Mom. And talking of Dad, it's not always me who has to play the grown up. This is why I hate...'

Aksh was cut off mid sentence as his uncle walked up to them. He put his arm around Aksh and said fondly, 'Mr Mehra, this is my sister, Reena, and my nephew, Aksh Soni, the famous one in our family. He has been more than a son to me through this wedding. Aksh, this is Ajay's employer. Mr Mehra has given Seema and Ajay the most marvellous wedding gift. An all-expenses paid honeymoon to Koh Samui. It is in Thailand. Really, Mr

Mehra, thank you. I cannot tell you how excited Seema is to fly overseas for the first time in her life.'

His mom folded her hands in a greeting and Aksh volunteered a handshake to the lean, fair, well-dressed gentleman in expensive rimless glasses, 'Pleasure to meet you, Mr Mehra. That is a wonderful gift.'

Mr Mehra looked ill at ease as he mumbled, 'Ajay deserves it. He works tirelessly for the firm. I believe you are a writer, Mr Soni?'

'Yes and please call me Aksh.'

'Only if you call me Raoul.'

'I will leave you all to chat. Please excuse me.' His uncle sauntered off leaving the two men alone. Aksh inspected the room through the corner of his eye, looking for Sia. He needed her social graces to bail him out of the pressure of keeping the dialogue going. He felt a sense of alleviation as she gravitated towards him.

'Sia is as pretty a name as the lady herself,' said Raoul smoothly as Aksh introduced him to Sia. The guy was a charmer but not in an unpleasant way. Sia glanced at Aksh, visibly charmed. 'So do you write too, Sia?'

'No, Raoul, I am a graphic designer,' she replied.

'So it is a meeting of the visual and the verbal, I see. Unfortunately, I am lacking in the creative department. I view the world in out-and-out logic and reasoning which is my wife's major grouse towards me. Aksh, she would be thrilled to meet you. She is into all things bookish. Oh! Speaking of the horned one. Don't tell the Mrs I said that,' sallied Raoul as he put a finger to his lips.

'Raoul, should we go get ourselves some dinner?' Mrs Mehra's voice made an entry before she did.

'Sure babe, but I want you to meet someone. I was telling Aksh here, that you would love to meet him.'

The lady in reference looked distinctly familiar. She was clearly charismatic although perceptibly apprehensive. Her hand dazzled with rings, as she extended it in greeting. It hit Aksh at exactly the same split second as Raoul said it, 'Karin. Aksh Soni and Sia.'

'Hi Sia. Hello, Mr Soni. What an honour to meet you! I loved your book but I am sure you hear that way too often.'

Aksh was nonplussed. It was decidedly her. He looked straight into her supplicating, kohl-rimmed eyes and played along with the charade. If this is what she wanted, then this is what she would get.

'Thank you, Karin. It is very kind of you to say so.'

While Sia and Raoul swapped parting formalities, Karin turned to Aksh, smiling and mouthed a thank-you. Her almond-shaped eyes shimmered under the brightly lit chandeliers. Then she was gone, arms linked with Raoul. The one thing he had to give this woman, she knew how to make an appearance.

# 8A

Dear Aksh,

That was weird on all counts. Sorry, I did not know how to react. I got caught on the wrong foot. I was flustered and before I could figure out what to do, you were consigned to being a stranger.

Karin

P. S. Sia is pretty.

# 8B

Karin,

Knock, Knock.

Who's there?

It's me.

Your gateway to your muse.

Never ignore your muse when it comes knocking. That was Writing Tip 1.

Relax. I get it. Yeah, Sia is pretty. Raoul seems like a nice guy. My uncle was full of praises for the generous Mr Mehra, who enviably, was so at ease in a suit and in the setting. I, on the other hand, am impaired by stuffed shirt syndrome of a different kind. The bondage of a suit and tie becometh not the bohemian quintessence of a penman. Fifty shades of grey is not my style but Hell hath no fury than a mother and girlfriend scorned, so I dress my best in family affairs, which ironically bring out the worst in me.

To cut a long story short, our brief meeting today resuscitated me out of the monotony of the proceedings, so it is all hunky dory. There was drama, there was suspense. Notwithstanding you obliterated my presence, I forgive you. Speaking of cryptic actions, let me see if I can clarify the ambiguity of mine. Karin asked and I quote, 'Why are you even bothering with me?' I have no concrete answer to that. Let me put it this way—it will be refreshing and reviving to go back to the process of initiation of a book, without the performance anxiety associated with my own efforts. I no longer have the luxury of that flexibility when I write. I sense that you have a book in you and it is a rousing stimulant to help kick-start it into action. Then there is the ego boost of being the glamorous Ms Karin Mehra's object of veneration. That is my clandestine incentive in all of this. Do not overthink or soon I will too, and then it is a lose-lose for both.

This is exactly why I never write under the influence of wine, women or song. It brings out the rambler in me. See? We all ramble. I am still stuck here at the wedding. I think my paranoia is building as people keep making not-so-subtle suggestions that Sia and I, head the Ajay and Seema way. That much abused and overused aisle is so full of potholes that I can hear the screams of those who have fallen into the trap of marriage and cannot escape. Wait! Is that you I hear?

You know, I kind of get why you have swatted the writing bug for so long. Your life is running at breakneck speed. Slow down, shut out and get on with it. Gather ye rosebuds while ye may. I think I am beginning to master this mentor thing. Practice makes perfect in almost everything, except alcohol. That sneaky ambrosia of seduction is infallibly the boss.

I am high. I am bored. I am sorry for this meandering piece of tripe and will understand if you want to boot me from my job.

Cheers!

Aksh

# 8C

Dear Aksh Soni,

You are quite the court jester. I think humour becometh you. I am being dragged by my hair, kicking and screaming, to another social engagement. I hear you. Yes, you are right. I have no time or bandwidth to pen a word of any consequence. Your job is under no jeopardy. Do not resign. I promise to get down to it. I have to go. Thank you for understanding.

Warmest regards,

Karin Mehra

# 9

# The After Party

'I diot! Idiot! Idiot!' Karin berated herself. What was the big deal if she had confessed to having met Aksh earlier? 'Idiot!' What a fool she must have looked like, acting like a tongue-tied teeny bopper! What a freakish coincidence! Aksh's good-humoured reaction was some sort of consolation, at least.

Karin still felt on edge, wanting to curl up and hide. She needed to go home. She shuddered when Raoul's arm made contact with her body and she quickly put her cell phone away.

'Sorry, babe! The men were all queuing up in the loo like piddling was going out of fashion,' Raoul slurred.

'Raoul, can we go home instead? I am really in no mood for more hobnobbing with people. I have a system overload,' whined Karin.

'Karin, we have to drop in for half an hour. Sunil will kill me. And your dear friend, Payal will obsess about your absence from her grand anniversary party for the rest of your life.' Raoul raised his fingers in a quotation marks action. 'Only a quick drink. I promise.'

The driver swung in with the car. Raoul reached out to help Karin into the car but she chose to snub him.

'And you don't consider this unreasonable? This is nonsense, Karin! I am trying to keep it light!' Raoul snapped irritatedly.

'And, Raoul, we both know the reason for your fine spirits, literally!' retorted Karin.

The thing about drivers is they master the art of being unobtrusive. The Mehras paid their drivers handsomely so they were more suave in the skill of being discreet than most of their ilk.

'Driver, head home!' Karin snapped.

'Driver, Shiro's, please.' Raoul raised his voice.

After waiting for a few seconds till the tug of war finished, the driver followed the last set of orders. Shiro's it was, he gauged. It was a rudimentary but foolproof formula.

'Karin, are you menopausal or what? These mood swings are getting too hard to handle!' Raoul tried reasoning with her.

'Everything about me is not menstrual or mental, Raoul. You men always seem to think our hormones are the culprit. I do not want to go. I am dead beat. I do not give a shit what anyone thinks. Worrying about people, answerability, doing what's right, saps me no end. There has to be an expiry date to all of this. I think if I went to Mars for ten years, even twenty, and came back, nothing would change. The women would still be wagging their fingers in the air to flash their diamonds. The men would be bragging about the killing they made in the stock markets. It should be called a talk market, the amount of talk that revolves around it. The underlying theme of each party will remain the same. Mine is bigger than yours! This is what life is whittled down to? Stagnation!'

The driver turned up the volume of the music.

Raoul tweaked her nose and laughed, 'Ha ha ha! Talk market? That's funny! There is a flight to Mars in the near future. After I make some more money in the talk market, I will book you on it. Listen, let's not drag this on. I don't know what's upsetting you but we are almost there, so I suggest you put on that adorable Karin face and once you have a few drinks, you will loosen up and this will pass.'

'You know, Raoul, I think the driver has a better idea of how to handle matters than you!' Karin knew this was going to lead to a nasty backlash but she was beyond caring. She also knew this was going to be a lengthy night.

'Screw it, Karin! I will see you inside. Tell me when you want to leave. Since I seem to be getting on your nerves, I suggest you stay out of my way so we don't make a spectacle of ourselves.' With that, Raoul stalked out of the car.

Karin wanted to kill someone. She knew her reactions were out of proportion but she could not care less at this point. Maybe Raoul was right, she was acting like a menopausal bitch. Or her immature conduct while meeting Aksh was getting to her. She wanted to rewind the night. This was exceptionally wearying and now Raoul was going to be in no mood to reconcile easily.

In this state of mind, Karin entered the party. Her sari and smile both in place, ever so stylish and not a drop of the deluge of her inner chaos was allowed to rise to the veneer. Shiro's was one of the largest restaurants in Mumbai and Karin wanted to lose herself in the expanse but the place was plastered with guests in every nook and cranny. Nobody in Mumbai missed an invite to be seen at happening parties. Everyone wanted to be a part of the happening crowd at the happening lounge bar. Karin detested the use of the word in this context. The happening hosts, Sunil and Payal stood at the entrance under the protection of the imposing Buddha standing tall above them which cut across both levels of the restaurant.

'Karin! Darling! Thank you for coming! The dance floor has been so dull without Raoul and you!' Payal looked exceedingly joyous to see them.

Karin resigned herself to her fate and ploughed into the swamp of society. Air kissing, hugs and compliments on X's outfit and Y's groundbreaking diet. Women in Mumbai seem to have a genetically implanted fat scanner. You've lost weight. You've gained weight. It was usually the start and sometimes the end point of many a meeting. Pink champagne flutes levitated through the crowd. Karin drank one, then another, and then she stopped counting.

She sashayed her way to the bar where Raoul, Sameera, Myra, Sunil and Payal were chatting. The DJ, like a mini version of the Buddha minus the repose, was stationed above the dance area. As if on cue, he started spinning retro disco tracks.

'"Mamma Mia!" Now that's what they call music! Hey guys, I know why they call it bubbly. It does exactly that to your mood because I feel so bubbly! Myra, let's go!' Karin consciously avoided Raoul and seized Myra by the hand, dragging her to the dance floor.

Karin, at her tipsiest, could give any youngster a run for her money. The dance floor and Karin had a long-term romance. The music and her body moved in tandem, in hedonistic rhythm. Myra tried to match moves but was too gawky to pull off Karin's fluidity. The tempo changed to a love song. She glanced at the bar but Raoul was nowhere in sight.

'Come, Myra. Let's get ourselves a well deserved glass of champagne!' Myra followed Karin meekly.

Sitting on the bar stool, Karin tried to spot Raoul. He was engrossed in an animated conversation with Sameera, their dinner plates resting on the table. Sameera's bosom was dribbling out of her blouse and it was not with the milk of human kindness. Her hands kept touching Raoul's and even from that range, Karin could see Sameera playing her 'playful, giggly girl' card and coming out trumps. Raoul met Karin's gaze and then wilfully chose to look away. He said something to Sameera who laughed and brushed his thigh.

If there was one thing Karin knew about Sameera, it was her attention-monopolising behaviour with men. She would not share the limelight with any other woman. The men were putty in Sameera's touchy-feely hands. Rajiv, Sameera's bland husband, was in awe of his trophy wife so he was satisfied that he was the one who got to go home with her at the end of the party.

Directly in her line of vision appeared Maninder. Manny, as he was called, was infamous for his silk shirts and dance moves. Manny was covertly nicknamed such, because of the many rolls of beer belly comprising his humongous waistline. Add to that, slim-fit shirts and a bhangra number, and he had an Axe effect of a different sort. Women wanted to axe him and his sweaty body, which was in dire need of a deodorant, but he was one pesky chap who could not take a hint. His wife rarely came to parties because she was a simple woman who felt out of place in this scenario.

'Let's dance, Karin. Why are you sitting alone, alone? You were staring at the dance floor so I said to myself, Karin wants to dance but is feeling shy to ask.' Manny had a smug smile resting placidly on his stack of double chins, as he came closer. His shirt button had burst and released a layer of fat into unhindered view. He was a pestilence that could not be swatted easily but Karin's preoccupation had made her open target for the many moves of Manny.

Before Karin could gather her wits, Myra jumped to her rescue, 'Want to get a bite, Karin? Everyone is eating.' Karin almost fell off the stool in her dash for safety, thanking her lucky stars and Myra. They gathered their plates and Karin went towards Raoul's table.

'Hey Karin! Come join us! Your husband is such an entertaining man. Never a dull moment for you, I am sure!' Sameera crooned.

'You bet, Sameera! He definitely has the gift of the gab.' Karin said with saccharine sarcasm.

Raoul narrowed his eyes, knowing trouble when he saw it brewing. Myra went for another helping, pulling Sameera along for company.

'What in God's name is wrong with you, Raoul? You insisted on coming for this party so I can dance and eat alone while you sit and purr sweet nothings in Sameera's ears?' Karin hissed.

'Karin, you really are on some trip. You walked off leaving me high and dry. What was I meant to do while you were busy gyrating on the dance floor? Don't turn this around on me. Sameera happened to be there and we got chatting. So sue me!' Raoul was livid.

'Screw you, Raoul! No, in fact, go screw Sameera!' Karin snarled back.

'Karin, you have one hundred percent lost it. You have been itching for a fight ever since we came here. You were set on ruining this evening. And speaking of drinking, look who is talking! How many have you knocked back, Mrs Pious Mehra?'

'Hey lovebirds, get a room.' Sameera's cloying voice sliced the tension, leaving them suspended in mid rage.

Raoul waited for Karin to finish her dessert.

'Shall we leave, Karin? I have a conference call, early in the morning.' Raoul said with a poker face.

'Noooooo. Don't be a party pooper, Raoul.' Sameera urged them to stay.

'Yes, Raoul. Don't be a party pooper. Let's have a glass of champagne.' Karin signalled to the waiter to do the needful.

'I am done with my quota for tonight,' Raoul said unyielding.

'Well, one for the road then.' Karin guzzled her champagne in a shot.

'Let's go, Karin.' Raoul steered her away from the waiter.

They said their goodbyes and held on to the decorum of wordlessness, in the plush interiors of their vehicle.

The driver knew this was the most explosive state. This unnatural stillness. He drove swiftly, wanting to get away from being caught in the crossfire, as fast as he could.

The kids were back home and Raoul went to wish them goodnight. Karin's head was spinning. She abhorred the thought of another altercation with Raoul.

He changed into his pyjamas and then with icy composure, said, 'Karin, I really have no clue as to what is happening with you. You are overreacting to everything I say or do. I am walking on eggshells with you round-the-clock. Honestly, it is exhausting. The kids are awake so I suggest we discuss this tomorrow, if you want. Or you can carry this on, like you have been doing all evening. Either way, I am going to sleep.'

Before Karin could respond, Shanaya came barging into the room.

'Mom, you promised to help me with my project!'

Karin regretted gulping that last glass of champagne in haste. Somehow she managed to sound lucid and go through the motions. Luckily, Shanaya did not notice how her mother's hands shook as she cut the pictures for the project, a task she usually did, with such precision.

Morning, afternoon, evening, night, come hail, wind or storm, Karin, the mother, could not let her kids down, although she could barely stand up herself.

# 9A

Dear Aksh,

The wise man, Confucius once said, 'One drunken rejoinder deserves another.' Chances are, he never did but I wanted to sound scholarly. I am pissed and pissed off. The former piss is a state of part delirium and part wild abandon. The latter piss is a state of ire that usually afflicts the much married. There is a third piss but it is too unladylike to elaborate on the definition of that one.

Like the classic conundrum of 'what came first, the chicken or the egg?' do we get pissed off because we are pissed or do we get pissed because we are pissed off? Now that was confusing, not to be mistaken with Confucius. I would like your esteemed opinion on this debatable topic.

I am drunk, cranky and irritable, all at once. I am fed up of breezing in and out of 'happening' parties. I am sick of air kissing people I can scarcely tolerate. I am bored of playing the other half of the 'life of the party' couple. I am beyond fed up of bringing up kids who blame me for all the fatal flaws of their inherent, biological configuration. I want to throw up. I want to have another drink. I want to be unencumbered like you. You, who is living my dream.

Cheers to that!

Yours spiritedly,

Karin

# 9B

Dear Karin,

I can only imagine how arduous life must be for the 'haves' of the world. This unencumbered Aksh chased his dreams in the local railways, not a Mercedes, and they came with a price. You have beauty, brains and bucks. Struggle, my dear, real struggle, the 'have not' style, is what you need, to give edge to your objective. You have not been sharpened enough on the millstone of life, so you view it myopically. You are born with a silver, no, a diamond spoon so even your troubles seem to be tragi-glamorous. One of those scandalous housewife narratives may well be your forte.

Tonight, we will both go to sleep, feeling drunk and doomed. The only difference is, it is easier to toss and turn on a bed of roses than it is on a bed bug-riddled mattress. Renown and riches do not always go hand in hand.

Night after night, in my waking dreams, I break into a cold sweat. Images and sounds flash, titillating me. These concubines of imagination want to be brought home into my stories. I bring them respectability by giving them my name. Then they wait, pregnant with ambition. Waiting to be flaunted in front of the world, bearers of my inspiration. I skulk around in shame, waiting for acceptance.

That is what it feels like to be me.

You still want to write, Karin? Quit whining and pining. Do it. Write.

You asked for me as mentor. For better or for 'verse' you got it.

Aksh

# 9C

Aksh,

You are a mean drunk. What do you know of me? All that glitters is not gold or that which sparkles is not diamonds. What makes you so critical anyway? What lies beneath the maverick, malcontented mask? Granted that you are leagues ahead in the writing department but it does not qualify you to pass judgement on me. Let's turn the tables here. You are not that different from me. What is that you lack on the personal or professional front? You, Mr Soni, want to portray your life as tragi-struggle. Are you worried that if you luxuriate in your meteoric ascent, you will lose that underprivileged edge, so you hang on to that sharp blade of hostility?

You know, Aksh, let me tell you a secret. There is no women's liberation. It is a fallacy. The best of us, be it working women or homemakers, lie prostrate in the face of motherhood and domesticity. That is the yardstick of womanhood. Society has craftily embedded this muzzle. No matter what we achieve, how much we struggle to keep pace, eyebrows are raised if a child fails an exam or a husband does not get home-cooked meals. That is our measuring cup and we sink in this well of conditioning. Take this friend of mine, the CEO of a multinational conglomerate with a billion-dollar turnover. Her son is a drug addict and each of his misguided life choices is attributed to her career. Women are constantly walking the tightrope of conscience-stricken ambition, teetering in our high heels, to strike a balance.

The reason I have waited this long to pursue writing, Aksh, is not because I was socialising, but because I chose to be a mother and wife. Emancipation has shackled women into superhuman expectations—a tribe of beauteous behemoths who undergo rigorous training in the art of multitasking. Do you know how much is invested in parenting? All of me. For twenty-plus years, 24×7, with no breaks. I am unsure if the extent of that sacrifice is valued by either my husband, children or society. I am quite sure it made no visible difference in the macro picture. Though I can tell you, those moments were precious, even if transient. That has been reward enough, in a sense. However, through the passage of all these years, my brain has been simmering steadily on the back burner of responsibility. Before it is charred beyond recognition, I need to write this book for myself.

I am sorry if I overstepped my boundaries here but I am not going down without a fight.

If you are drunk, I am drunker.

Karin

# 9D

Whoa, Karin!

That was one feisty comeback! I see there is a raw, plucky side to the polished Mrs Karin Raoul Mehra. Point noted, Your Honour. I am culpable as charged, of insensitivity. In my defence, I view things from the perspective of a male and an author. The primitive stereotype of provider, dogs a man every step of the way. Writing carries the stigma of being a not so lucrative career choice. We wordsmiths are warriors. We believe in our craft and are inclined to battle convention, to be able to do what we love. It takes guts to reach for that elusive glory. Better late than never, Karin.

It has been an evening of full disclosure and it did cross my mind whether I should throw in the towel or take up the gauntlet? The dispute of to be or not to be your mentor, did arise but I get a buzz out of honesty. How about we call it truce? No judging the other, henceforth. What happens in Vinoland stays in Vinoland.

One word of counsel. Never bite the hand that reads you or your future tome.

I am going to get the last word in.

I shall sign off and meditate on your 'piss and pissed off' quandary.

The creative caveman,

Aksh .

P.S. You are pretty sexy when you are hopping mad. Forget I said that.

# 9E

Aye, Aye, Captain. Truce.

Karin

P.S. I am pretty sexy all the time. And you are not so bad yourself. Forget I said that, too.

# 10

# The Agent

Aksh chose a casual t-shirt and flip flops on purpose. It was not the appropriate attire for the meeting but Aksh needed some control over the circumstances. Jim Patel alias Jignesh Patel was Aksh's puppeteer. Like all agents, the strings of Aksh's success were orchestrated by Jim. Since childhood, Aksh had noticed that some people had explicit animal features. Take Simi Aunty. She definitely looked like a donkey. The upper teeth breaking into a Shrek-like smile. It always astounded him when she opened her mouth to speak. He almost expected her to hee-haw but true to form, her laugh did sound like a bray. In the same vein, Jim Patel was the human prototype of a weasel, through and through. His sinus issues did not help his cause. His nose, always twitching and sniffing. His small, watery eyes, always shifty and darting suspiciously. The unifying factor these hybrids shared is that their personalities matched the nature of their external beast.

The transformation of Jignesh Patel to Jim Patel was evident in the choice of locale. An upmarket deli now formed the setting for his meetings with clients. A glass of wine always tastes better when served by pretty waitresses. Far better than his fledgling client discussions at Udipi restaurants, loudly slurping on Madras coffee served by an oily waiter, with his pinky finger raised in the air. Jim had the hide of a rhinoceros and the tongue of an angel.

This matchless amalgamation had soon raised his stock as one of the most in-demand agents in the business. Aksh knew he was fortunate to have Jim but he could not help despise him from time to time.

Just off The Gateway of India, the Colaba deli was bustling as usual. The glass displays of exotic cheeses and cold cuts lay in wait, diagonally opposite the dessert counter, all with fancy names and prices to match. A melange of women having set-menu lunches, huddled in gregarious groups. Corporate head honchos with their laptops, getting a quick-fix power lunch. The odd tourists who unabashedly adhered to their guidebook recommendations. And the incessantly punctual Jim Patel.

'Hi Jignesh,' grinned Aksh, deliberately using the full form of his name.

Jim shook his head and offered Aksh some wine.

'So Aksh, any breakthrough in the new book? I have three publishing houses asking to name your price.'

'I am not a factory for mass production, Jim.' Aksh enunciated his abbreviated name emphatically. 'I will start working on the book as soon as I have sorted my ideas into a coherent whole.'

'Ya. Ya. I know you well enough by now, Aksh, so I have been stalling them with promises. False, of course, but it keeps them salivating for more. Just get moving Aksh. The public wants more of Aksh Soni. You are a lucky son of a gun but of course I did have a teeny-weeny role in the making of the man and future legend, if I say so myself,' boasted Jim.

'Yes, Jim. Try as I might, if I wanted to forget your contribution to my noble cause, you would not let me forget. Now what was the urgency of a face-to-face meeting?' asked Aksh.

'You know Tapanlalji and Bapanlalji?' asked Jim.

'Who? Those Bollywood dudes with all those hideous back-to-back hits? Are they twins or what?'

'Yes, Aksh and no, they are not twins. Hideous in your opinion but the audience thinks otherwise. Listen, I met a big boy from their office and guess what? They are open to the idea of you scripting a film for them. Can you imagine what this would do for your career?'

'Are you kidding me, Jignesh Patel?' Aksh spluttered. 'I cannot even approve the screenplay adaptation of my first book after five rewrites and you want me to write a script for these clowns. I am an authentic author. I write in English. I do not think in Hindi. You want me to create characters who dance to item numbers with heaving breasts and also have substance? I detest Bollywood and its steady stream of mindless trash. Sure, if push comes to shove, I can manage to write a Bollywood script but does it captivate me in the least? Perhaps, after I have had a lobotomy. My answer is a resounding no! Is there any part of that, you do not understand?'

'Aksh, I understand everything. It is *you* who is not comprehending the future. How many books do you need to write and sell to get anywhere close to making the big bucks? Books have many enemies. Piracy, e-Books at 99 cents, movies, the internet, smart phones. Let us not disregard the new writers that are sprouting like weeds in the market. All these are erasers that are leisurely wiping out the written word as you know it. Wake up. Be vigilant. Be smart. What am I here for? To squeeze the luscious juice out of all your success, while you have it. This is my job. You get the bang for the bucks you pay me. The more bucks you make, the more I make too. Do it for me. We are joined at the hip so stop trying to fight it,' said Jim smugly, his weasel nose moving habitually.

'I tell you what, Jim. Translate this for me, Bollywood style, and you win this round. Try it. "The rain drops wore their glass sheathing and launched themselves at the unsuspecting passersby." Treat this as a line from my script for your two *jis*. Go ahead. Try it.' Aksh crossed his arms and smirked. The wine was so smooth. He swirled it in his mouth and let it caress his throat, as it went down effortlessly.

'Let me translate it for you, Aksh. You are thirty-five plus. You need money, like other ordinary people, however extraordinary an author you may be. It does run out, you know. There is no guarantee of how many books you will churn out in your lifespan or whether people will want to read them. How do you even know if your next book will be a bestseller? The burden of writing is yours and the outcome is unknown. In films you get paid, regardless of the outcome of the film. Others carry the weight, once you deliver the goods. Why don't you look at it this way? Let celluloid pay for your passion. Most of us have to be practical first and then we can follow our ideals, when that slog over is done. You, unlike us, have fulfilled your dream, so now get real. Unless going back to doing your Masters and then doing your nondescript professor bit, at this point of your life sounds like a better Plan B. After tasting first blood, you think you can go back to that? You can still try and win your Booker-Shooker prize, you know. This is just side income.' Jim defogged his glasses and took a sip of his wine. Handling Aksh was like dealing with a juvenile delinquent. Rebellion was a staple on the menu.

Aksh felt the floodgates of fear creaking open, as he had a certain flash of memory. 'Dad, I do not write to earn, I write to exist.' The naïveté of that statement, in hindsight. As much as he hated admitting it to Jim, he realised with a jolt that he took the perks of fame for granted. Impermanence was going to be a permanent feature, where monetary matters were concerned. That necessary evil, money, offered two sides of the same coin, entrapment and ensuing autonomy. Then it was back to the drawing board and the cycle would continue.

'What was your dream anyway, Jim?' inquired Aksh, now more than a tad tipsy.

'Acting. I won consolation prize in the fifth standard for best actress. In the history of Fatehchand Boys' Academy, nobody got so many claps for playing the role of a beggar woman,' said Jim proudly.

'Why the hell were you playing a woman's role anyway? There was a school like this? Where?' exclaimed Aksh.

'In Rajkot. It was a boys' school. No girls. Everyone thought I should have won first prize but the teacher liked the boy who was acting as a famous ballerina. I should not be saying this but it seems the teacher had tendencies, if you know what I mean. I really deserved to win. Everyone said so.' Jim looked like he was going to cry.

'It is never too late. Your Tapanlalji and Bapanlalji can give you a role in their film. Then everyone will call you Jigneshji. Hey! You will be like 3G!' laughed Aksh.

'Anything is possible, Aksh and you will be the one to write a role for me in your screenplay?' Jim glibly countered. 'There is a party for the hundredth-day of their film and I have been asked to bring you along. Give it a thought. Bring Sia too. My swear, just come.'

'My swear? Who says that anymore? Oh yeah! My mother does! Okay! Fine! Just so you stop pestering me and let me enjoy this wine. I will come and do a tap dance, Bollywood style, to the tune of Tapji and Bapji but I am not committing to anything. Is that clear?' said Aksh assertively.

'Loud and clear! God swear, no pressure.' Jim beamed.

Jim Patel gulped his wine in a shot, glad the ordeal was over. If Aksh had the power of the pen, he, Jim Patel, had the power of persuasion. And a bottle of fine wine.

# 10A

Dear Karin,

How are you doing, hot mamma? I thought of you today. Not in the way you think! Got you there didn't I? Oddly, while I met with my agent. Surprised? Don't be. This process of writing is an undefiled exercise till you decide to share it with the public. Then the vanity of vocabulary leads you into a cesspool of commercialisation. You are sucked in, and getting out is not even an option. Write for the love of it, not for the money or the repute. It is a dichotomy to think that we, as writers, need isolation and then adulation. Is it any wonder that the streak of insanity runs like a fault line through our accursed ilk?

I got to be the golden boy 'Aksh Soni' on my own steam. What irony that now I need to be manoeuvred. Bollywood, here I come, dancing and shaking my pelvis. Yeah. That is my agent's grandiose scheme for us to get wealthy and stay wealthy. My new manuscript can be called *Jhatka Matka* or to give it a more savvy flair. *Dolly Sood in Bollywood.*

This is where I come back to why you crossed my mind at the meeting. Do you know horse racing parlance? Sometimes an owner enters two horses in the same race. He can only expect one to win so the other horse runs as a pacemaker. The pacemaker sets the pace so the fancied horse is spurred into blazing a winning sprint. Send me your ideas and I might be able to bolt from the starting point too. You be my pacemaker and I will be your mentor. Sounds fair to me.

Am I putting you off the business of writing? Then get out now while you can or enter at your own peril, Karin. Do not say you were not warned. If you are still adamant, then procrastination is unacceptable. Now get cracking before I start cracking the whip. Be my deliverance.

The Equestrian

# 11

# Raoul and His Band of Boys

The crows were smirking as they daringly dipped their beaks into the leftovers on uncleared tables. The Cricket Club of India had a waiting list of countless applications for membership which had earned it the nickname of The Coveted Club of India. Their formidable doors were closed to people but these cackling creatures could swoop in as and when they pleased. The sadistic black-hearts would deliberately fly in the path of enthusiastic walkers. This was their domain and they marked it with total aggression.

While watching the green immensity of the lawns, Raoul waited in the colonial lobby. The modernisation of the club was intentionally left incomplete to retain some of its original character. Adding to its lofty ambience, was the grand piano near the main entrance. Raoul liked coming in early and listening to the pianist deftly playing classic tunes. Most of the people around him were senior citizens, who despite their hearing aids and walking sticks did not miss this weekend performance. Even if their senses had dulled, their appreciation of music remained eager.

Sunil was on time as usual. Harry and Vijay walked in a few minutes later. Rajiv was running late and was not sure if he would be able to make it.

They moved to the bar, as was the routine. After ordering drinks and snacks, the men got down to business. They had been discussing starting a venture together.

'So continuing from last time, I spoke to my buyer in China and he insists there is a tremendous future in packaging. He has the machinery and we could import it at cost.' Harry was a good businessman and knew the ropes.

'Who will run the show, Harry? I am neck-deep in work. I don't mind the investment but...' asked Raoul.

'Leave that to me, guys. I have enough men at my factory who will be able to handle day-to-day administration. The lazy slobs need to earn the fat salaries I pay them.' Sanjay interrupted and dismissed Raoul's qualms with a wave of his hand.

'Raoul has a valid point, Sanjay. We are not talking of management but of leadership. With the size of this project, one of us should be willing to give the time to oversee the business,' said Sunil. He was closer to Raoul as compared to the others and he knew that Sanjay's brusqueness got to Raoul often. 'Perhaps Rajiv might take on a stronger role, so should we just hold this conversation till he gets here. Is he coming today?'

'Harry, why not have your contact send us a detailed report which we can discuss at length when all of us are present the next time? I am in too, if the numbers add up,' offered Vijay.

'Fair enough! Let's drink to that. I raise a toast to China, via Bangkok.' Harry winked suggestively. 'Now that we might be in business together, let's try and mix pleasure with it.' The men turned towards him trying to figure out if he was serious. 'Stop looking at me that way, guys. It's not like you have never thought of cheating on your wife,' he paused dramatically before adding, 'But what if your wife cheated on you?' Rajiv walked in at that point. 'Rajiv, I do not want an answer from you. Sameera has you wrapped around her finger.' Rajiv rolled his eyes and grabbed a beer. 'Me, I am safe. Myra is scared of her own shadow. I don't think she will have the guts to have an affair. That's why us men were given the balls, so we could use them!'

'I don't know, man. Who thinks of this stuff? The only affair Veena might have, is with her jeweller in exchange for diamonds and I buy her enough of those. After paying the price for her blood diamonds, if she did actually have an affair elsewhere, I would dump her in a second and cancel all her credit cards!' Vijay said decisively.

'I would kill Nonita and she knows it. No mercy! A slow, horrifying death if she screws with me.' Sanjay threatened.

'All those hours Payal spends at the gym with those six-pack trainers of hers, I would hire a beautiful secretary or two, and give her a dose of her own medicine. Raoul, you are left. What is going to be Karin's punishment for infidelity?' asked Sunil.

'I would forgive her,' Raoul said simply. Looking at the disbelief on the face of the men, he explained, 'If Karin had an affair, there has to be something missing in our marriage. I have to accept some responsibility for the situation. I must have failed somewhere if she needed to look elsewhere. Also, I am not a fool. There is no way I can manage the girls or the house and all that she handles. So, all this time invested in marriage, and at this age and stage of our lives, I have no intention of rocking the boat.'

'You are more henpecked than Rajiv!' laughed Sanjay.

'What? I am not henpecked,' protested Rajiv.

'Call it what you want, Sanjay. To each, their own. Frankly, like Sinatra, I do it my way,' Raoul said coolly.

Sunil butted in. 'Good one, Raoul! Bored of this topic now! Where are the drinks? Let's get down to the real stuff that will never leave you high and dry. I raise a toast to all toasts.'

The other men started discussing the project with Rajiv but Raoul's mind was straying. As he played with the rim of his glass, he thought of Karin. He had tried to provide her with everything but was it enough? To see her happy, made him the happiest, but somehow he often felt he was falling short. Lately, she was so closed that he felt like an outsider. What if there actually was someone else? Would she be able to throw away all these years of marriage? At the end of the day, they were a team. He would never leave her because he did not know how to live without her. Unless...unless she wanted it that way. Raoul's logical mind was unused to delving this deep into conjecture. Ripples of discomfort passed through his head and his natural defence of compartmentalisation kicked in. Yes, it would hurt like hell if she was unfaithful, but he would definitely forgive her. It was a hypothetical question. It had been answered. And that was that. Finishing his drink in a shot, Raoul got back to business.

# 12

## The Mirror

L ately, it was the ladies' toilet which she wanted to avoid at all costs. Why is it women always migrated to restrooms in pairs or more? Karin was thus far to see a man ask another man.

'I am going to the toilet, want to come?'

What a silly formality! Yet it was such an intrinsic female protocol. In those restrooms, the women would sneak calculating glances at each other through the buffers of the mirrors, age no bar. They were reflecting surfaces to each other, cruel in their transparency. As they grew older, Karin noticed the chinks in the armour of youth gone by was highlighted with the scarlet lipstick that sadistically ran down their beyond middle-aged lips. The lipstick, the red rag to the charging bull of time. Each crack trumpeting, 'You are old!' Only a more age-devastated woman's mirror image would bring some alleviation, as she dextrously tried to cake her wrinkles with the deception of foundation.

Karin stood in front of her bedroom mirror. It was her décolletage she hated the most. The French had loaned a resplendent word, effeminate and annihilating. The tiny creases that were creeping and mysteriously multiplying overnight. She held her breasts close and the rivulets of age surged into rivers. Line after line. Then Karin distended her face. The mongoloid features that took shape, nauseated her furthermore. The grey hair that had started voraciously devouring their black brethren, reminded her of frizzy pigeon feathers. She pinched at her erstwhile svelte legs. They used to glow with a sleek sheen and took pride of place in Raoul's erogenous zone preferences. They were now reduced to nothing but a flabby storehouse of overlapping shapelessness. Karin could not bear to see her face nor her body. Crow's feet, turkey chin, bat wings, the whole menagerie of middle age, in one cellulite-encapsulated zoo of lard. She felt enraged towards Raoul, towards all men. Wives are just lumps of meat with housekeeping abilities. Husbands are like meat extractors. They chew off itsy-bitsy chunks till only the fatty parts are left. Fatty parts that nobody wants.

This vitriolic brooding was arousing a massive migraine. Why had she become so hypercritical and pessimistic? She reasoned with herself. For her age, she was in decent shape but to expect her body to be the same size and shape, twenty years later, was asking for the moon. As for her face, let Botox be the panacea for all evils, like it was for most of her friends. Up to now Karin resisted the Botox Brigade or the Liposuction Line-up. It all seemed pathetic, this useless crusade to turn back the clock. Irrespective of their face-saving experiments, women around her all looked like clones of each other, with their perennially startled expressions. The Miss Universe 'I am so amazed' facelift or 'The Cat Woman would be envious of my feline eyes' alternate option.

Karin felt like opting for an induced coma right there and then. Her mind was like the archetypal dog chasing its own tail and making no headway. If this mental state was like writer's block, she had to break down each letter of the alphabet to make sense of all the madness coursing through her. Technically, if she had not written a word of worth so far, was she still eligible to resort to the writer's block diagnosis? Was this even making sense? She had to find her bearings. Where to begin? Till her insides were purged, nothing was going to help. Responsibility had a stranglehold on her dreams and she needed to break out of its restrictive clamps. She was interred underneath the offal of domesticity. Her inner voice was hoarse with all the shouting for extrication. If one could hear the devil, he would sound like this silence. Overpowering and never-ending.

Lately, Raoul had been doing a lot more entertaining in a bid to expand his business interests. Her role in the girls' lives was nuisance value. They just about needed her and clamoured for their privacy. She felt redundant and wanted to retrieve her lost years. Years spent in motherhood and running a superlative home. The sneaking suspicion harried her constantly that it would have played out pretty much the same way if she had chosen a professional path. Housewife. Homemaker. Most tête-à-têtes ended after you furnished that as your primary occupation. The socially adept ones would veer the chat towards irksome domestic staff and the rigours of educating children. Then throughout the evening, irritability would play discordant notes like broken guitar strings ricocheting in her head. She had toyed with the idea of therapy but that too had become a badge of honour for the Botox Brigade and therefore repugnant to her.

Karin tried meditative exercises a few times, pushing her mind to wander from its wanton destruction. Did Aksh genuinely find her appealing? He did not seem like that much of a ladies' man. Not bad, Karin Mehra. *My secret lover, Aksh Soni.* Would his hands touch her body with as much artistry as did his words, her mind? Guilt whacked the thought, almost as soon as it materialised. What was his day like? How would a working author spend his day? She could not imagine him complaining about the consistency of the teriyaki sauce or analysing the fluctuating trends of the stock market. He could not possibly be entangled in the mesh of routine. Or could he? How is that with Aksh, she could dismantle herself into the most unorthodox thought processes and venture forth to express most of them? Why could she not envisage having the nerve to reveal herself with Raoul like she did with Aksh?

The main door shut with a toned down clack. Raoul was back. Karin jumped into bed and pulled out a magazine from her side table. The mirror stood tight-lipped, an amenable co-conspirator in her secret thoughts.

'Hi there, babe. Sorry, I am late,' Raoul lisped perkily. 'These guys are thinking of a joint investment in China which seems to have a lot of growth prospects and you know how it is. . . .'

He chucked the car keys and his phone on the bed. It was a habit that drove her batty. Why couldn't he place them on his bedside in a civilised manner? He sprawled on the bed with his shoes on. His breath reeked of alcohol and his hair seemed to be wreathed in an invisible halo of cigarette smoke, discernible only by its odour.

'Did you smoke? Jeez, Raoul, how do you guys even remember your alcohol-fuelled business discussions, the morning after?'

Raoul kneaded her abdomen. Bad idea. It made Karin squeamish as she felt the folds of her copious belly oscillating under his hands. He touched his fingertips to her face and tried to trace the outline of her lips. Karin inched her face away so his hand dropped back on the pillow.

'Chill *na*, babe. Why are you so cheesed off lately? Talk to Daddy,' he slurred, as he continued his rubbing motion on her thumb.

Karin shirked away and turned her back to him.

'Go to sleep, Raoul!' she said in exasperation.

He put his arm around her and it felt like the albatross, bobbing to the sound of his tractor-like snoring. In a bit, Karin took off his shoes. Like a rag doll, he raised himself as she made him wear his pyjamas. He opened his drowsy eyes and pouted his mouth into a kiss. In the blink of an eye, snuggled under his blanket, he was asleep again. She kissed his forehead lightly and contemplated the peculiarity of men, of how both barbarian and baby are harboured in one testosterone-filled body.

She adjusted and readjusted herself, entreating the fugitive sleep, that so seemed to favour Raoul. Somehow, everything seemed to favour Raoul. His eyelashes rested heavily on his face. His eyelashes were the envy and joke amongst the women. No amount of mascara could give you Raoul's layers of keratin-blessed eyelashes which lustfully draped his honey brown eyes. His boyish good looks had withstood the test of time, creditably. As much as it got under her skin constantly, as a matter of fact, Raoul wore the requisite armour of rationality to ward off the blows of her intensity. She dozed off imagining a Venn diagram. In one circle was Raoul and rationale. In the other circle was Karin and emotion. Somewhere between the paradox of their personalities, lay their tenacious zone of harmony. Karin sensed there was a tornado spiralling menacingly above them. A tornado named Aksh Soni and it was so easy to be carried away in his whirlwind of words.

# 12A

Dear Aksh,

Are you flirting with me? I am a married woman. Remember? So behave yourself. But thank you for the 'hot mamma' endorsement. Now back to your proposition. For a second out there, I wanted to run for the hills at the demoralising projection of writing but the thought of you penning scenes of couples in love, dancing around trees, brought me back to my senses. I cannot possibly leave you to your own devices. It is not every day I get the chance to be pacemaker to an author. However, I do believe you may be giving me more credit than I deserve.

Do you ever enter a library and feel dwarfed by the magnitude of books and the glut of authors? I do. I berate myself and feel ludicrous that I can ever imagine my name being a part of that hallowed portal. I feel like an imposter in this world. The stories have been told. The words have been said. Where am I to find one that will be read? Then I come across an epic book and its magnificence enthrals my senses like a narcotic. I weep because I am so moved. I weep because I will, in all likelihood, never write that way. And still, there is not a shred of misgiving in my mind, that I have to write. I want my books to be the torchbearers to my legacy. That seems so pompous an idea, so preposterous, even as I say it.

I see-saw on the blade of insecurity. On a given day, I believe I am born to write and then on another, I feel every idea is plagiarised from the library of recollections nestling in my subconscious.

I am daunted, as much as I am haunted. Aksh, you might be backing a lame horse but I can promise to try and give you a run for your money. Expect your first instalment of 'The Karin Chronicles' in your mail, after I am done dusting the cobwebs.

Running scared,

Karin

# 12B

Dear Karin,

You are bright and beautiful. I hold you accountable for bringing out the bad boy in me. Next time he gets out of hand, I will punish him and send him to a corner of the room. Happy?

Coming to your bibliophile neurosis—you are not alone.

When I read and reread drafts of my manuscript, it felt like I was hallucinating the originality. The boundaries get fuzzy after a while because the lines of our own material and those of other writers seem to get cross connected in our heads.

I reckon we are all handcuffed to an electric chair of unworthiness. Us, creative ones, even more so, strapped like mummies. If I were an artist, I would illustrate a surreal depiction of a writer, recurrently stabbing his brain with a serrated nib. Each oozing wound leaking a story of pus and gangrene. It is candid and fundamental because it comes from passion and renders the misery inconsequential. Readers are cannibals and of our own volition, we obligingly feed them portions of the trilogy of our minds, bodies and souls. Sometimes they ingest the taste, but usually they spit us out and our bones rot in the sun of dismissal. We are damned if we do, damned if we don't. We are tortured.

Deliciously,

Aksh

# 12C

Dear Aksh,

That was macabre and elevating, in equal measure. Can I tell you something eerie? Recently, I had a similar cannibal metaphor about men. Ask not in what context. Trust me, you do not want to know. Do not mind my nosiness but do you share this kind of self-doubt with Sia? Merely curious.

The Copycat

Karin

# 12D

Karin,
Curiosity killed the copycat.

Aksh

# 13

# The Exchange

Dear Aksh,

Inhale. Exhale. And here goes. I take my first step into the deep end.

*'Roy never seemed to smile. He did, undercover, when he could bare his fangs and howl at the anaemic, full moon. In the platinum glow, yes, that is when Roy smiled. Then he met her. Her chestnut skin brought out another strain of animal in him. To tame the beast within or lose her. Both sides of the coin flipped destruction.'*

That's it! The nutshell that you asked for. Well? I have a few more ideas but I will let them loose gently.

Yours considerately,

Karin

# 13A

Dear Karin,

Ummm. As your aquatic instructor, you have the correct style but vampires and werewolves do not make a splash. Simply put and I apologise for the critique, this theme is been there, done that and then some more.

Throw me another. I will know it when I see it.

Sorry.

Aksh

# 13B

Dear Aksh,

Ouch! I tried a free shot, hoping it would pass. I chose my mentor wisely, so rejection will come with the territory. Here it comes. The next assault on your senses. Be lenient but not too lenient.

*'She was antagonistic towards her mother. This was the time for Naomi to have boyfriends and get drunk. Not the other way around. Then along came Jay. The like poles repelled each other even further as the magnet of Jay attracted both mother and daughter.'*

I feel like I am back in school waiting for exam results. Am I foisting this trauma on myself out of choice?

@Mycrystalball @Akshsoni When will my ugly duckling pond of words turn into a bewitching swan of a book?

Yours nervously,

Karin

# 13C

Karin,

I have bad news and good news. The bad news is that the concept is a melodramatic cliché. The good news is, I like your technique, the sampler I have seen of it.

I am not certain if you are conversant with Hemingway's *tour de force* of brevity. Six words that propel the nuances of a story to an immaculate conception.

*'For sale: baby shoes, never worn.'*

I use this as a benchmark when I begin anything. I have no such genius but it is important to be earnest (pardon the lame pun, too hard to resist) and fanatical about this preliminary process.

Karin, where is that story? The one you accused me of stealing? The one that will blow my brains. I have a very strong hunch that you were not referring to the decoys you have sent. Come on. Out with it. Swim over to this side and stop paddling around in the shallow end. Unless I am totally wrong, which I rarely am, I am prepared to bet you are saving the best for the last. So dilly-dally no more. Time is of the essence here. I will settle for nothing less than that story you are holding back.

Aksh

# 13D

Aksh,

'Everyone called her Uncleji's pet but only she knew how accurate that phrase was. In large joint families like hers, the eldest male member was accorded deity status. Revealing his feet of clay would topple the edifice of their familial home. So she prayed religiously to all the gods in the family temple to strike him down with their arsenal of divine weaponry but even the gods remained quiet.

Her uncle adored her for as long as she could recall. She was his blatant favourite amongst all the cousins. She returned his affection equally. Her baby hand enclosed by his on family outings. Her innocent stories, to which he would give a patient and compliant ear. Her father was an apparition that coasted in and out of her childhood, perpetually in the background.

It all changed that day. Maybe it was the same always but perhaps she felt it then. Like an arrowhead, the memory protrudes. The swing in their garden was her treasured spot to play. Uncleji called out to her. He was swinging, higher and higher. The women were cooking in the kitchen. In the twilight, Uncleji put the little nine-year-old girl on his lap. He encircled his arms around her waist and pulled her close to his body. She chortled as the swing bobbed and swayed. The girl felt something as solid as a pebble through her polka-dotted cotton dress, so she shifted a bit. Uncleji held her closer and nuzzled her neck. She turned her face towards him, confused. He smelled of eau de cologne. He was sweating. His eyes were glowing. He was scary. The hardness under her was making her very uncomfortable but Uncleji had her in a vice-like grip and kept pushing her down. She tried to *wriggle away but he put his arms around her concave chest and kept pinching and massaging it gently.*

*"I want to go to Mamma," the little girl cried.*

*"See if you are not going to sit without fidgeting, I will have to punish you." He spoke in hushed tones as he pinched her a wee bit more brutally. "If you tell anyone, your Mamma and Papa will die. What have you been taught about obeying elders? God punishes disobedient children."*

*The lights came on in the house and someone called out her name so he reluctantly let go of her. She ran and ran till she was out of breath. She could see the lighthouse in the distance. If only she could drift to it and clear her head in the cold water. Her mind was totally confused. She hated Uncleji. She did not know why but from that point in time, she truly did. If anyone noticed the change in the girl, they did not broach the matter.*

*Her cousin got engaged shortly thereafter. Uncleji was unwell and offered to stay back and look after the kids while the older ones and their parents went for the confirmation ceremony. He put his five-year-old nephew to bed. The girl was asleep, unknowing of the caretaker that her parents had chosen.*

*Uncleji covered her mouth with his betel leaf-stained fingers and lay her spread-eagled on the bed with a towel beneath her. She resisted and resisted and cried and cried but he kept telling her how much he loved her. As he parted her waif-thin thighs, the excruciating pain and her tininess forced him to stop. He offered her his "lollipop" instead. A special, magic one, he whispered, as he forced open her small mouth. His eyes were ablaze, as he stroked her tear-stained, sticky face again and again. The taste of Uncleji has never left her palate till today. That sea water and metallic taste. That gagging. Her uncle's inheritance.*

*She never did tell anyone. Like the lighthouse, she stays taciturn and unreachable. She had chosen to be Uncleji's pet. It was her fault perhaps, at the end of it all.'*

Karin Mehra

# 13E

Karin,

Now that is a story! Move out of the way, Hemingway, it is Karin Mehra's turn! It is hard hitting, gut wrenching and thoroughly disturbing. Disturbing is good. Writing has to move people to reaction, reaffirmation or revulsion. I would love to read more, once you have developed it. I mean that. I do not have much time on my hands so my replies are not exactly fast-track. Let that not deter you.

Despite the fact that most stories have been hashed and rehashed, it is the treatment that decides its fate. From your letters and this piece of work, I sincerely believe you have what it takes. That spark that sizzles. I had that once too. Now it is barely a flicker. Stay true, Karin. This is the only time you can. The grass is murky and muddy on this side of the fence. Speaking bluntly, my fair lady, I was vacillating about whether I wanted to be Henry Higgins to your Eliza Doolittle. The desperate housewife captivated my inquisitiveness and in a 'what the hell' moment, I responded to your first mail. Writers are parasites of observation. We feed off the natures of people, sponging off the material of their lives. I needed to see what makes you tick, half expecting a neurotic stalker. My motives were less altruistic than I let on, I admit. By now, I would have hemmed and hawed my way out of this, but I am a sucker for a great story. Yours meets the requirements.

Go the distance, Karin. Find the horsepower to race this thoroughbred to the finishing line.

Aksh

# 13F

Dear Aksh,

Characters flit through my head like sprites in a fairy tale. They string colourful ribbons of words and swirl and twirl, till I tie them into pretty bows of various hues. I hear them in that enchanted forest of limitless possibility, waiting for me to return. Each twist and turn changes the landscape into a kaleidoscope of opportunity. I am their Pied Piper and they will follow me to the ends of the Earth. They trust me to emancipate them from the cavernous recesses of imagination.

I have been lying to myself forever and ever with this candy floss version of inspiration.

In actuality, each time I lunge at a word or a character, it sears my head, branding it like a vial of concentrated acid. There is nothing remotely pretty or fairylike about it. I hear a roar that commands me to release it. I shun it because I am afraid. I am afraid if I write, I will face the darkness of the woods within me. I am afraid of myself.

I want to be a princess but I am Medusa with the serpents of memories, coiling and hissing, waiting to strike, inwards.

The Devil has decided to take up everlasting residence in my head. The fires of hell blaze within the nucleus. I wear rings on my fingers, birthstone rings, evil eye rings, rings depicting magnanimous gods but I still stew in the venom of despair. A slow, agonising burn. I want to douse the feverish inferno with the cooling release of the words that are repeatedly kindled in this crematorium of memories.

I do not write because I am a coward so I skulk around for scraps of stories.

They say everybody has a book in them and mine is a mongrel dog, teeth bared, who feeds off the carrion of my past. If I come too close, it will rip me to shreds. So I run and hide, closing my ears to its ceaseless growling.

I am not Alice in Wonderland.

I am intensity, tempered in the hot coals of pain.

I will burn all those who come too close.

I cannot tell this story, Aksh.

Help me find another.

Please.

Me

# 14

## Bollywood Bash

'Aksh, it's Jim. He wants to know what time are we going to reach the party.'

Aksh muttered under his breath as he nicked himself while shaving, ruffled by the suddenness of Sia's query.

'When it's over, if I could have my way!' Aksh yelled across the room.

'I am telling Jim we will leave home in half an hour. Okay? Aksh? Okay?' Sia was exasperated with Aksh's unflagging grumbling about the Bollywood party, that Jim had stupefyingly browbeaten Aksh into attending.

'Yeah! Yeah!' Meet the twin terrors, Tapanlal, Bapanlal, have a couple of quick drinks and beat a hasty retreat. Aksh was not giving one inch more than the basic minimum attendance of his required roll call.

Sia had saved him the hassle of finding something suitable to wear and laid out his clothes on the armchair. He opened his mouth to argue about her choice of shirt but she pre-empted him.

'Aksh, if you are going to the party for a purpose, don't sabotage it with a thing as petty as what you choose to wear.' Sia knew how to navigate her way around Aksh's obstinate streak.

'How does what I wear affect how I write? I am a writer, not a wannabe actor! They never heard of "don't judge a book by its cover"? These Bollywood moguls could do with some reading so they stop doling out trash to the public, in the name of cinema,' Aksh retorted.

'So here is your chance, Aksh, to bring about a revolutionary change in the film industry. Enter Aksh Soni. The man with a sensible script.' Sia cajoled him. 'Now tell me, how do I look? Do I look fat?'

The trick question that has badgered men across continents and cultures was at Aksh's doorstep to answer. Sia looked radiant in her off-white tunic and palazzo pants. Her hair tied in a chignon, highlighting her turquoise hoop earrings.

'You look fine. You look so fine that the terrible twosome may offer you a role in their next film. Then you can support your impoverished writer boyfriend and bring home the bacon.' Aksh joked.

'Very funny! Come on, let's leave, Aksh, while your sense of humour prevails. I am relieved you are not being that much of a grouch about this. I expected a battle royale. There is hope for you. For God's sake, do not spend the evening scowling and surly,' said Sia.

'Scowl? *Moi*? Gasp! I will be like Little Jack Horner who sat in the corner,' Aksh retaliated mockingly.

Sia grabbed hold of his hand and led him towards the door, before he got a chance to change his mind. Aksh stomped his feet in a mock tantrum before yielding and following Sia to the car.

The party was at the poolside of a midtown five-star deluxe hotel. The entrance was groaning with the tonnage of huge hoardings of the hundred-day wonder film. Aksh felt the gestating cloud of a bad mood but Sia clasped his hand

and he decided to grin and bear it. A motley crowd of people thronged the place. The starlets, the press reporters, the behind-the-scenes team and gatecrashers were segregated by their lowly location at the pool. Additionally, there was a heavily secured party room. Bouncers stood at the door and unless you were worth a pretty packet, famous or recognisable, entry was prohibited. People were pushing, shoving and baying for the bartender's service in the commoner section.

'Sia, I refuse to join that blaring mob. You are going to have to wait for your drink unless you spot the weasel.'

'Weasel? Oh! Jim! Aksh, you are nutty! Anyway, I do not want to drink.'

'Eh? How are you going to pull through the night without alcohol? Where is that cartoon network anyway? Must be licking someone's white shoes,' Aksh guffawed. 'There he comes, the Rambo of agents, Jimbo!' Sia pummelled his arm playfully.

The luminosity of Jim Patel's Thai silk shirt made him stand out in the midst of the crowd. He walked towards them, sniffing and beaming, simultaneously. He handed Aksh a glass of sangria.

'At last! Sia, looking lovely as usual. Thank you, for suiting and booting your boyfriend properly. This man will give me a nervous breakdown.' Jim joked.

Sia laughed. 'Been there, done that, Jim!'

'Jim, along with the cockroaches, you will outlast a nuclear disaster, forget nervous breakdown. And we both know it!' Aksh rallied back.

'I am not sure if that is a compliment at all, Aksh, but time for frivolities later. Let us go meet Tapanlalji and Bapanlalji.' Jim led the way.

Aksh grumbled and put his hands to his forehead in an exaggerated gesture, eliciting hearty laughter from Jim and Sia.

'Aksh, you are such a drama queen sometimes!' Sia said affectionately.

'What is a Bollywood party without histrionics?' Aksh said chirpily. 'If you can't beat them, join them. Lead me to the gallows, Jim.'

'The Almighty be praised. The reformed Aksh Soni, keep up the masquerade, for a while longer.' Jim heaved a sigh of relief.

The bouncer moved away to let them pass into the unassailable shrine of the celluloid syndicate. Jim had his *'setting fit,'* a catchphrase he flaunted often.

The hype of exclusivity was downgraded by the cheesy velvet sofas. The flaxen spotlights advertised the muscle power and glamour quotient of stardom, that was circulating around in the decadent setting of the room. Those without beauty, the brains, were immersed in sermonising in sporadic huddles around the place. The star-struck waiters were serving drinks liberally. Breaking loose from the madhouse outside, felt like an acquittal and Aksh wolfed down another sangria. Then he was ready for the up, close and personal encounter.

'Sir. Sir. This is Aksh Soni.' Jim at his obsequious prime, tried eagerly to break into the circle surrounding the hosts.

'Come, come, sit. Have a drink.' Tapanlal, or was it Bapanlal, gesticulated to the server, who almost tripped over himself to get to them promptly. 'So when are you writing a golden jubilee hit for us? Jim *Bhai* has praised you so highly.'

The doppelganger sibling added, 'Yes, yes. We must do a film together. Any ideas, Aksh *Bhai*?'

Aksh *Bhai*? Thank God, Sia was not part of the goings-on or both would have burst out laughing.

'Well, Sir. I have never written a novel with the intention of turning it into a film. I write about real people and their real problems. I leave it to you to make it from real to reel.' Aksh responded.

'Yes. Yes. You English writers are very smart but you must not forget one rule. We Indians, have an appetite for spice, so we need *masala* in our food and films!' Brother Number Two nodded solemnly, in agreement.

Back to Brother One, who seemed to be the team spokesman. 'You come to office with Jim *Bhai* and we will have a story sitting. Now you enjoy party. Was pleasure to meet you.'

An aspiring starlet was orbiting the perimeter around them. She had oxidised rings on her fingers which disoriented Aksh. It was a Karin trademark, those rings on most of her fingers. The similarity ended there though. The girl was too vulgar. Despite her youth, she lacked Karin's vulnerability, her vigour.

The brotherhood eventually noticed her. 'Sneha is your good name? This is Aksh *Bhai* and Jim *Bhai*. Come sit, sit.'

Sneha's pancaked face elongated into a jumpy smile and then she quickly diverted her attention back to the star makers, as she found a spot within the circle of influential men. Aksh grabbed the chance and Jim's arm, moving away from the centrifugal forces of the party.

'See Aksh? How people are waiting for this chance and it fell into your lap. Now write and let us make money.

How awful was that? You always create a commotion, unnecessarily!' Jim said indignantly.

'Jim! Shut up! Enough with the shop talk. I deserve a drink.'

'Go have your wine, Aksh, and circulate, circulate. It is as vital for your career, as blood circulation is for your body. I will see you later. I have to meet some people.' Jim left as they approached Sia, who had been texting on her phone.

'So how did it go?' Sia asked.

'Do you remember our walks at Marine Drive, Sia? Back in the day when we would watch those monkeys performing tricks, when animal rights protests were nonexistent. The monkey man had that fixed bag of tricks. Come on Charlie, dance. Come on Charlie, be a watchman. Come on Charlie, shake hands. Then that wretched, pitiable monkey would beg for alms, goaded by the fear of the stick that had engineered his performance. I now realise the poignancy of that selfish simian show. The meeting, it went somewhat like that, except I did not turn somersaults.' Aksh replied dolefully.

'Cheer up, Charlie. Was it that bad?' she said compassionately.

Aksh laughed wryly. 'Operation Codename Charlie went exactly as expected. For East is East and West is West and the twain shall never meet till Jim Patel brokers the deal. Not sure. Who knows and who cares! It does not matter. Why aren't you drinking? I am going to get one. Want?'

Sia nodded her head in the negative.

Aksh got his drink and plonked himself on the sofa beside Sia. He looked at her probingly.

'You look flushed. You sure you have not been drinking on the sly?' he joked.

'Frankly speaking, I carry a hip flask, Aksh. One of the many cloak-and-dagger things I keep from you, but you are always too preoccupied to notice. How do you think I have put up with you for so many years?' Sia's eyes twinkled in mischief.

'Sia. International woman of mystery. The lush who loved me.' Aksh chuckled. 'What an idea, Sirji!'

'And the sequel could be called Aksh. International Man of Mystery. But did he ever love the lush? Therein lies the true mystery,' parried Sia.

Aksh did not or chose not to notice the sudden onset of rancour in Sia's statement. An act of omission was easier to defend than an act of admission. It was a rapid downhill ride after that and the night was over before it had begun. Both knew it. Neither discussed it. It was always better that way.

# 14A

It was the most radiant red bush of flowers I had ever seen. Its haughty beauty enhanced by the anomaly of its surroundings. It grew proudly on the railway tracks. My heart in my mouth, at the thought of passing trains decapitating its incorrigible buds. I was a passerby. There would be many others. That she stood upright, taller and longer than any of us, gave me hope for its imperishability. The resilience of its spirit set it apart from all the pretty flowers blooming in mundane gardens. Now I have a name for those fiery blooms. I will call them Karin.

Aksh

# 14B

Dear Aksh,
*Tragedy finds its solace in stories.*
*Unheard, they shed tears of blood.*

Karin

# 14C

Dear Karin,

*The flame beckoned the moth.*
*Its fluttering wings in Death's dance.*
*Nonetheless it took the chance,*
*for that warm light it sought.*

Aksh

# 14D

Aksh,

*Many a time she wished someone would steal the moon.*
*No endless nights of loneliness, waiting for the sun to rise soon.*

Karin

# 14E

Karin,

*Scared of losing it all, she was afraid to speak her mind.*
*Only after she set her words free, herself, did she truly find.*

Aksh

# 14F

Dear Aksh,

*I will follow you into the gloaming.*
*Into the light.*
*Reel me in with your words.*
*And I will follow you to the other side.*
*I promise I will follow as you lead.*
*There's no place to go but here.*
*My barge of doubt and fear,*
*I leave, for you to steer.*

Karin

# 15

# The Children

Amara was twenty. Shanaya was sixteen. The chronological noose of those years has spared no parent, including the Mehras. Raoul was the chilled out dad while Karin was the nagging disciplinarian. This perception was writ large in the girls' unabating altercations with Karin. She wondered when her daughters had turned into these tempestuous torrents of tirades.

Eat healthy. Study for your exams. Sleep early. Clean your room. The full monty of motherhood was stripping Karin bare of respect from her children. Raoul had quick fixes for all problems and Karin felt like handing over the reins to him for just a little while. Talk was cheap when one was rarely home and got to play Daddy at the dinner table and in front of the television.

When they were clingy children, she was waiting for them to grow up and be independent. Independence in the children came with a price. Their baby talk turned into bombastic squabbles. Not a week passed without a showdown. Karin was tired. So very tired. Motherhood should come with a disclaimer like 'the images of respectful, submissive children portrayed in certain books and films are fiction' or 'child rearing is injurious to your health and sanity'. They should put this on birth control devices so people know what lies ahead.

Imagine a condom packet portraying a screaming teenager and a crestfallen mother. A drugged minor ignoring his anxious parent's phone call.

No reprieve. No respite. Only this constant tussle. Yes, Karin was mentally exhausted.

'Psycho! You are a fricking psycho! Get off my back and go get a life. Stop controlling mine!' Amara, her first born, the most pristine love she had ever felt, that Amara.

Karin's tears welled up as flashes of that baby girl in the cream lace dress hovered around, taunting her. That placid girl who would hang on to each word of each storybook, her mother read to her at bedtime. Amara's poems were a source of pride and joy for both her parents and teachers alike. Only when Amara was asleep, did Karin find traces of her missing child. She was hidden under the blotched mascara and mini skirt of this twenty-year-old banshee.

'Don't you dare talk to me like this, Amara! What is asked of you? That you stop wasting your time just partying and drinking, and do something constructive? Read, you loved reading. Write, you were so good at that. I can get you an internship at...'

'Mom, why don't you get yourself a job instead? So you stop getting on Shanaya and my case.' Amara scathingly cut her mid sentence. 'You keep saying you stayed home to look after us. Now we have grown up, so there is no justification anymore! Because you want me to write does not mean I will do it! I am old enough to do what I want. Stop suffocating me!'

'Amara, I am your mother. It is my role to guide you, to worry about your future. What is wrong with you? Why have you become like this? Even Shanaya has started misbehaving, watching your rude behaviour.' Before the words left her mouth, Karin knew they were a mistake.

'Mom! Why are you involving me in this! You have a fight with her and get irritated with me! Leave me alone!' Shanaya screamed.

Amara slammed the bedroom door on Karin's face and yelled, 'Nothing is wrong with any of us! Something is wrong with you! Go ask Papa too! Everyone in this family complains about you!' Amara's words were saturated with hate. Unadulterated hate.

A maelstrom of tears, hurt and memories inundated Karin and she rocked herself to get a hold on her unnerved mind. Time lost its concept as she stayed that way, rocking back and forth.

She did not even realise that Raoul had entered the room till he turned on the lights and gave her a quick glance. She shielded her swollen eyes which were stinging from the harshness of the light.

As he removed his tie, he said, very casually, 'Amara called at the office today. She was very upset. You know Karin, you need to stop micromanaging the girls. They are at that age where they are going to rebel. I suggest you take it down a notch. Hands off, babe, hands off.'

Karin's voice shook with controlled anger and anguish. 'And Mr Raoul Mehra, I suggest you take over handling your darling daughters. Wait up for them till they reach home at their tipsiest best, after their club hopping! Dial their numbers till your fingers hurt but they never answer and your head aches with worry about their whereabouts! Watch them throw away their talent! Go one step further and please share a drink with them every night. That should really bond you further. The Tippling Mehras! Drunken stupors are our act in this circus, we call home!'

'Quit removing your frustration on me, Karin! Don't make this about you and me. They are spot on with what they are saying. You have been acting bonkers lately!

Nobody is after you. You are starting to sound like you have a persecution complex!'

'Why don't you yell louder, Raoul, so your cherubs get some more ammunition to shoot accusations at me? Do you know how gruelling it is? Do you have any darn idea what it is to be in my shoes? Twenty-three years of life, my youth, have gone into being a wife and mother. You think I cherish this anymore? What do I have to show for it? You got to be the breadwinner. Money does not talk back. It grows, verdant and ripened, waiting to be spent. The fruits of your labour are sweet. The fruits of my labour make me want to choke!'

'Of course, Karin, making money is a walk in the park,' Raoul said sarcastically.

'I challenge you to deny it gives you some thrill, some joy, some gratification, Raoul. What do I get for all that I have put into these girls, into this marriage? A card on my birthday and Mother's Day to make up for the rest of the year? Did you even hold me and tell me you understand how much it hurts to be treated with such contempt, by my own children? When is the last time you said that I made some microscopic contribution to the man you are today? Has even one of you ever told me that twenty-three years of my life has been worth something to someone in this family? What is worse, I know superficially I have everything and yet there is an immeasurable void. It is like there is a can of worms infesting me, eating away at me, slowly but surely. I know I should be counting my blessings and I do, but I am lacking something larger, that is all mine, something greater than the mediocre average of all these thankless roles I play.'

'Calm down, Karin. They are your kids. They are works in progress. Remember our days of youth? I am sure we put our parents through this misbehaviour too. I refused to cut my hair for months, wanted to pierce my ear, get a soaring eagle tattoo with the feathers running through my shoulder blades. Did I ever tell you that? My folks wanted to disown me. Subsequently it all pans out. Look at us today. You know they do not mean it. Chillax, babe. What is it you want to do?' Raoul moved towards her in a reconciliatory gesture but Karin moved away, maintaining the gap between them.

'No, Raoul, stop patronising me or do you believe I need to be mollified because I am a psycho, as our dearest daughter just called me. I have also been diagnosed with a persecution complex by Dr Know-it-All Mehra. As you can see, I am incapable of calming down. I am also fed up of pouring more of my life down this black hole. I was young and smart once. Not much of me is left anymore. I am going to reclaim whatever I can, in whatever time I have left. For starters, I want to write my book. I want that leeway, guilt free. I need to write my book. I need that means of release.' Karin stressed empathically.

'What will you gain with writing, Karin? It cannot be for the money. That would be peanuts. If you feel like this, why don't you come and work at the office? We travel, we party, we live a good life. What needs of yours are not met? What you have done for the children is what all mothers do. Writing was a hobby you could have easily followed while managing the house and the kids. Why lay the blame on everyone else? Who stopped you from writing?'

'The call of duty stopped me, Raoul. Instead of writing a poem that was stuck in my head, I was helping with homework. Instead of jotting down a story idea that went by in a flash, I was making small talk and trying to impress your clients. It seems so trifling as I say it but it took all of me, the choicest of me. My mind is not on remote-control creativity, appearing like a genie from Aladdin's lamp, at my bidding. I never got the time or the encouragement and I plodded along, carrying the deadweight of my unconsummated dreams but always upholding this family first. None of you have respect or value for my input and it hurts. It hurts like hell. My life seems an exercise in futility. There was a time, the minute the girls would enter home they would rush through my door to share their day, chattering nineteen to a dozen, curled up against me. Now I have to literally break down the door to get one word in with them. Their reluctance to connect in any positive way with me is disheartening, to say the least. A hug or any act of endearment is beyond my wildest dreams.'

Raoul leaned towards her in another bid at pacification but instead it aggravated Karin further.

'As for you, I am the ideal hostess, dance partner, television companion and the entire ensemble. Have you ever considered the notion that I need to reserve a small portion of myself, for me, and not in relation with this family? This family cannot be the via media to my self worth. What am I doing here besides rusting on my laurels and corroding away in redundancy? So, do me one favour, Mr Raoul Mehra. When you come home, after enjoying more than a couple of pegs with your cronies, after you are done discussing who has been crowned king in the ladies or money dominion, after you are done with all that stock guy-gibberish, do not come and give me your crappy pointers on tackling the kids! Either take over the show so I can take up my hobby and please insert that word in inverted commas, *hobby*. Or be there for me because I spend all day picking up the pieces of this family, trying to be picture perfect when you come home, happy as a lark, after having being spared the torture of having to deal with any of this bullshit.'

'Karin...' Raoul started to say.

'No, Raoul. There is nothing more to say or hear. Do not waste your breath,' Karin said uncompromisingly.

They lay side by side for a while, her back turned to him. He switched on the television and started watching it in on mute. That irked her even more and she stormed out of the bedroom.

Karin spent most of the night reading in the study.

Not a book, not a magazine, but birthday cards, Mother's Day cards from her children, anniversary cards from Raoul, all which she had saved over the years gone by. And then, all the emails from Aksh.

# 15A

*You were sent to soothe my battered spirit's need.*
*An unexpected gift from the heavens, a miraculous seed.*
*Months and months of praying to the pantheon of Gods,*
*You survived, to justify my existence, against all odds.*
*Holding your frail little body, I swore,*
*I would love and protect you, from my very core.*
*Your dove-like smile soothed the lacerations of my past,*
*As you grew beautiful, inside and out and oh so fast.*
*Every desire, every need, my angel from above,*
*I fulfilled for you, who filled me with so much love.*
*But I guess, after the calm always comes the storm,*
*That, of motherhood, probably must be the norm.*
*The fights, the tears, the heartache,*
*So hard and oh so much to take.*
*The anger, the rage, the screams,*
*Crushing my hopes, my dreams.*
*Through it all, I have just one thing left to say,*
*I love you and would never have wanted it this way.*
*I tried, I tried and yet through all those tears, I cried,*
*I knew, for you, in an instant, I would have died.*
*I wanted for you what I never had,*
*To see us like this, makes me, oh so sad.*
*Just reach out for me, I'm always here,*
*To hold you and allay your every fear.*

*We will remain, mother and daughter, you and I,*
*But life's passing us by, in the twinkling of an eye,*
*Just hold my wrinkling hands and feel my yearning heart.*
*I need you, my child, because merciless time will tear us apart.*
*From the umbilical cord to the grave, we will be bound,*
*In you, I will eternally live and even Death's roaring call*
*will be drowned.*

Dear Aksh,
Does poetry count?

Karin

# 15B

Karin,

*'The talons of tyranny draw the blood from the words hiding like weaklings in my head, spilling the guts of a verse.'*

Poetry counts but not at the cash register.

Very poignant, I have to say.

I'm sorry too.

Aksh

# 15C

Karin,

Listen. I am giving a talk on writing. The invitation is in the mail. A little birdie tells me you could use the distraction, so why don't you come and behold my inadequate oratory skills? This is a once in a lifetime opportunity to watch me make a fool of myself in public. At least, it will guarantee me the applause of one person. You!

What say?

Aksh

# 16

# The Guest Lecture

'Together, we share the crutches of writing and walk as brothers in arms. It is here, we find ourselves, sometimes in the articulation of others.

Imagine a tree overladen with fruit, some ripe, some rotting. The branches buckle under the onus of their load. Only when the fruits fall or are picked, can the tree rejuvenate itself. You are like that tree, your branches will droop, pulled down by the heaviness of what you carry. You cannot replenish till you relinquish. Embrace your encumbrance. Find poetry in your pathos.

Writing is about WOE.

*Who On Earth?*

Who on earth will want to read me? Each foolhardy, striving writer faces this dastardly question. The established ones started that way too. Take my word on it. Consider this to be kindergarten in reverse. Writing comes before reading. Start being a writer now. Worry about finding readers later.

*Why on earth am I subjecting myself to this?*

Because we are afflicted with a disorder. We storytellers are manically addicted to our craft. We obsess with a word, an idea, a chapter. We compulsively look for the physical and mental arena to exonerate it. Let me take the poetic license of giving the big daddy '*Bard of Avon*' a Freudian twist. The fault is in our stars. Don't fight it.

*What on earth am I going to write about?*

The answer to that, my friend, is the most cumbersome part. Yourself? Your cross-dressing neighbour? Your three-legged hamster? I presume that some of you have read my novel. I am the '*slice my own balls and bleed them out on the page*' type of a writer. Does your strength lie in a *Game of Thrones*-like saga canvas? Or do you gravitate towards the light-hearted, frothy appeal of a *Mills and Boon*? Whatever works for you. Do not try and walk in another's shoes. You are likely to fall flat on your face.

*Where on earth did I come up with that?*

Throw away nothing. I am emphatic about this. Think of your phone, your laptop, your doodling pad as your granary. Store your grains. You never know which one germinates and sprouts into your story or belongs inside it. Do not, I restate, do not be disparaging or condescending to any abstraction, however bizarre or hackneyed it seems at the given point of time.

*When on earth will I begin or end this story?*

Begin now. It is like quitting smoking. It is not going to get any easier. The level of difficulty remains stagnant. The more you delay the inescapable, it can only be detrimental.

Ending your story. Is it too short? Is it too long? But my publisher wants 100,000 words. The ending is the proverbial Sword of Damocles hanging over our heads. Finish your core content and window dress corresponding to specifications. You have allies. The preposition, the conjunction and the adverb. They are the key to rescue you from the handcuffs of the infamous word count.

The keyword is WOE.

Writing is Whoring On Experience.

Our stories are illegitimate children of suffering. They are born of it and we suffer till we deliver them on a white sheet, staining it with our blood, sweat and tears. We need to give them their due, to give them their rightful place in the universe.

Spread the legs of memory. Thrust and thrust till your perverse pen orgasms into a creative climax.

That is my way of saying, write about what you know. Write because you must.

WOE is more than just a clever acronym. It defines us, on the page and off it.

This is Aksh Soni signing off. Over to you, audience.'

Aksh waited for the applause to die down. The standing ovation was embarrassing, to say the least. He felt like a sham, sounding all confident and looking almost swashbuckling. If truth be told, his knuckles were white, grasping the wooden panel of the speaker's box. He thought his rubbery legs would go under half way through the speech. He imagined his nerves, exposed and betrayed, like an X-ray on the giant screen behind him. Exposed to the audience that lapped up each professedly confident word he spoke. The deed was done and he was still in one piece. The more things change, the more they remain the same. That statement rung true, as he surveyed the auditorium. The moth-eaten, satin curtains, curbed by their frayed ropes. The gilded arches of the college auditorium, tarnished with neglect. What had once been so awe inspiring, was now humbled with time. The phone call last month, had been unanticipated and he tentatively accepted the Principal's humble and almost pleading request to speak to the students, in commemoration of the college's Founder's Day. The setting provoked a montage of the countless college functions, he had attended as a student, from talent parades to fashion shows, without fail on the fringe. The Aksh of today was a coveted trophy on the walls of alumni fame. Back to the future, here he was. From zero to hero. Pondering about the winds of change, he registered nothing of the Principal's vote of thanks, of the young student who conferred upon him a memento of appreciation, along with a bouquet of flowers. The wheezing static of the mike vaulted him back to the real world, to the here and now.

Had she come? That was his first thought, as the adrenalin sedimented itself. The audience looked like a collective canvas of bobble heads. Hands were raised in gusto to be the selected one. Aksh felt like Moses on Mt. Sinai, as he indicated at the bashful nerd, a dead ringer of his former college avatar.

'Hello, Sir Soni. I loved your book but I wanted to aks. Sorry, ask. How much of it is true? Like, how much of it is from your own life experience?' asked the bespectacled blob of jelly.

Sir Soni? Professor or Arthurian knight? Aksh was finding it hard to keep up a deadpan expression.

'If I tell you, I will have to kill you,' responded Aksh amidst the students' raucous laughter. 'When you write the genre of book I have, the foundation rests on a certain amount of introspective integrity. For example, I cannot write convincingly about claustrophobia if I have never experienced the fear of closed spaces. I hope that answers the question to your satisfaction.'

'Mr Aksh, your book is a predominantly male book and I enjoyed the insight into the male psyche. Can we expect a sequel which involves the man-woman relationship?' queried the girl in the neon blouse.

Aksh laughed. 'Women are an aesthetic riddle and it would take me a lifetime of acquaintance to decipher their entrancing depths. Never say never though.' The girl students hooted delightedly at his reply.

'Sir, I hear that your book is being made into a Bollywood blockbuster but are you able to write in Hindi?' asked the boy with the squeaky voice.

'As the song goes, I will get by with a little help from my friends in Bollywood. Thank you for the term blockbuster. That remains to be seen. It would help if you do not download it from the internet. Multiplexes offer sizeable discounts on weekdays and morning shows.' Aksh quipped.

As the laughter escalated, Aksh started feeling the duress subside. He decided to quit while he was ahead but not before his closing act.

Aksh scanned the front rows shifting his focus from the back rows. There she was. Her hand raised. This would be enjoyable. He indicated at Karin and announced that it would be the last question.

'Hello. I am not a student per se but I have studied your work and think highly of it. The title intrigues me as does your name. Can you expound on both?' Karin said impudently, recalling the frequency of that question at the book signing.

Aksh cleared his throat and decided to take the bait. 'Only if you tell me your name first, Ma'am and its meaning.'

'Karin Mehra. Karin means pure.' Her voice sounded husky on the mike.

He could picture her embarrassment as he pointedly said, 'Fetching name for a fetching woman. Regarding the title, *The Ancestral Skeleton* is how I view family genealogy, not just physically but also symbolically. I believe it complemented the subject matter of my novel. Now for your other question, the meaning of my name. It has many, but axis is the pivotal interpretation, pun intended.'

Karin smiled as Aksh and her eyes locked in an unwavering stare. Neither looked away. The cheers erupted and shook the room. The Principal prodded Aksh's elbow to escort him to the exit. Aksh waved a low goodbye and without breaking eye contact, he pursed his lips in a kiss towards Karin. Her eyes widened in alarm and her face looked flushed. Then, she hesitatingly raised her fingertips to her lips in reciprocation. He had this driving urge to jump off the stage and give her the bouquet of flowers but she had evaporated into the anonymity of the audience, just another bobble head.

# 16A

Dear Aksh,

Not bad, not bad at all. The friends and countrymen (undeterred by the absence of a few Romans) were eating out of the palms of your hands.

Thank you for the invitation. You were right. It helped to get my mind off things. It was an informative and absorbing talk. Take a bow.

Doesn't Sia or your family accompany you to these events? Or did I not see them? You do an excellent job of camouflaging your feelings. Who would have guessed the bundle of nerves lurking behind that zealous discourse?

Karin

# 16B

Dear Karin,

Hereinafter I baptise myself, Mark Antony Soni. Thank you. I am glad you came. I was not so glad when you were rattling the bars of my cage with your audacious inquisition. I should hire you as my mascot. You kept the goings-on lively. It marked the culmination of a harrowing session and all's well that ends well.

Sia was at work. My parents do not usually participate in these events. So, yes, it was just you, the only person in the audience apprised of my prior stage fright.

In its own queer way, as much as I gripe about these extra-curricular activities, I am happy for the interruption. Hanging overhead is the spectre of Mission Impossible aka my second novel.

Currently, I would even choose the horrible sound of chalk squeaking across a blackboard. A sound that marred my childhood years and ears, both. Anything is more bearable than listening to the soft, jarring click of the delete button of my keyboard, as yet another paragraph finds its way to the trash bin.

Aksh, The Garbage Man

P.S. You must be a great kisser. Just saying.

# 17

# The Homecoming Queen

Karin was a late riser. A habit she had slipped into, ever since the girls had finished school. Mornings were an unproductive period of time to be awake, with Raoul gone to office, the girls to college and the maids handling the household chores. Usually she read regularly through the nights but lately the rally of emails between Aksh and her, was her nocturnal recreation. She stirred and touched Raoul's side of the bed, as always. She saw a note, along with a yellow chrysanthemum on the bed. Raoul's cursive command simply read, *'Get dressed and enjoy the day ahead. Your coachman awaits.'* What was Raoul up to?

As she got into the car, the driver handed her three envelopes, marked numerically, along with instructions.

The driver refused to divulge information so she decided to stop interrogating him. Raoul was unresponsive to her phone calls.

The car stopped at its first destination. The Spa, as it was simply called, belying its lavish interiors, was famous for its therapeutic treatments. Raoul had organised a *'top-to-toe pampering package'*. A hot stone body massage, followed by a manicure and pedicure. Refreshed and revitalised, she opened the first envelope as instructed.

*'I hope my queen feels majestic and ready to rule the world.'*

Karin was so invigorated that her body and mind felt relaxed and she leaned back on the seat letting the driver lead her to the next stop of Raoul's plan.

The driver stopped at an antique store. A magnificent, Oriental, handmade ivory ship graced the centre of the eclectic store. Karin was flummoxed but when she entered, the lady at the vintage mahogany reception desk was well briefed about her arrival.

'Hello Madam. Welcome to ArtyFacts. Your husband has chosen a gift for you but he wants you to have the choice of exchanging it, if you so wish.'

Karin could not believe Raoul had gone through this much trouble. The gift was wrapped in handmade paper and Karin opened it carefully. It was a book, perfectly preserved. Her senses were heightened with exhilaration as she leafed through the first edition Enid Blyton. Enid Blyton! The beginning of her love story with books. Raoul remembered that?

'Would you like to see our other first edition copies, Madam? We have quite a collection.' The lady smilingly offered.

'Yes, I would love to but I am keeping this one. It is special,' replied Karin. The art deco cupboard was like King Midas's depository. For the next hour or so, Karin was awestruck. There were first edition copies of the Romantic poets to great Indian writers and a miscellany of autographed editions and proof-reading copies. Her hands shook with the excitement of gorging on these slices of history. It was unmitigated elation. Reluctantly, she left the store, clutching her precious gift in her hand. She meticulously ripped open Raoul's second envelope.

*'I hope my gift keeps alive the child in you, my lady.'*

Karin's eyes filled with tears. This was the most loving thing Raoul had ever done. The most priceless by a mile. She did not realise the car had reached home. It would be safe to assume this was her last stop since she had one more envelope. As she opened the door, it was pitch dark. It seemed as if nobody was home. That was peculiar. The strains of her favourite Gregorian music washed over the room. Her jaw dropped as she saw tea lights arranged on the coffee table. They were laid out so as to spell 'SORRY'. The incandescence flickered and leaped like ephemeral fountains of fire. They cast a supernatural glow on the glass vase which had yet another yellow chrysanthemum in it. Wrapped around the stalk of the flower was a handwritten paper. Karin increased the dimmer on the lamp and sat on the sofa. It was Amara's writing.

*'Dear Mom,*

*I know that in the recent years, it has seemed that all I have to offer is criticism, coldness and harsh words. Well, I think there is no better day than today for me to take a pause from our daily drill of arguing, to tell you this. Deep, down inside, I have always known I would be nothing without you. It is so ironic that the very things I criticise you for, are the things that make me who I am today. I am a perfectionist because you always taught me to strive for nothing short of the best. I am an achiever because you always pushed me to work my hardest. I am an individual because you taught me never to settle for being ordinary. You nagged me to write every time I did not want to and although I used to resent you for it, you gave me a gift I am very lucky to have. The greatest gift is to be able to express myself through my words.*

*I know that you put everything into bringing us up. I know you devoted your entire life to it. Every single project you stayed up till 4 am for, every party you threw for me, every toy store you spent hours in, every holiday you spent months planning—I want you to know I remember. I'll always remember.*

*I never thought how it must have made you feel when I constantly told you, as I was growing up, that all my friends* thought Papa was so cool but there's one thing I never got the chance to tell you. Throughout those years in school, my friends, teachers, parents, no matter who, the minute there was an impossible task at hand, they would say, "Tell Karin Aunty, she will make it happen." They spoke about you almost like you were some sort of a superhero, a wonder woman, some kind of sorcerer who could turn "no's" into "yeses"; be in ten places at once and create possibilities where there seemed to be none.

I feel so incredibly lucky that I can call that wonder woman my mother.

So, for all the times I have made you feel underappreciated or insignificant and for all the things left unsaid, I love you and thank you for being the unbelievably strong, fiercely loving, and absolutely incredible person you are. This one is for you, Mom.

The smell of fresh cookies wafts,
The lull of bedtime stories, gentle and soft.
The echoing laughter, bouncing off walls,
Watching the rain, as it falls.
Reading together, oblivious of the herds,
Lost in our personal world of words.
Innocence rifts like a soft feather,
Being tossed about in the breezy weather.
The sharp clash, of ego against ego,
Inflicting pain, blow upon blow.
The same words, now hurled like spears,
There's nothing left, no feeling, no fear.
The words manipulated, intended to hurt,
The exchange, if any, cordial and curt.
Tension moulds the air like clay,
And the wall just rises, higher each day.

*Subtle sweet moments, frozen in time,*
*Dancing shadows, playing like a mime.*
*Those years can be replaced by none other,*
*I miss the bond I shared with my mother.*

*Your recalcitrant Amara'*

Karin's emotions ran helter skelter. This was unbelievable. And unbelievably moving. And so crucially needed.

Shanaya's handwriting was still so childlike. Karin glowed as she read her younger one's letter.

*'Dear Mothery,*

*Since you like my "emotional terrorising" style, as you call it, and because it is what I am best at, I am going to stick to it while writing this.*

*You are very bugging. You nag me all the time, you shout so much and you drive me crazy. The End.*

*I am kidding. Now that I am done with the mandatory rude part, I will be nice to you.*

*Since I was a kid, I told you that I wanted to be a mother with a dimple when I grew up because you had those dimples in your cheeks. You have been someone I look up to from day one. Even today I want to be that mother with a dimple. As much as Amara Di and I never admit it, you are the strongest and most inspiring role model we could have ever asked for. We are so lucky to have you because I do not think anyone else will be able to compete with the values you have instilled in us or the upbringing you have given us. Even though you act like Hitler, you are a benevolent dictator because we are allowed to express what we feel and have our own opinions. That is something you do not find often.*

*I know we do not appreciate you enough and we never say those unrealistic, grateful statements that you keep expecting us to make but today I want to say this — Hey Mom, you know, you are really amazing, almost flawless. We acknowledge your effort.*

*I hope this made you laugh and cry. Jokes apart, I love you and I know I am your favourite child.*

*To My Mothery,*
*Like a hen, soft and feathery,*
*Watching over her coop, with love and care,*
*Even when you want to tear out your hair.*
*You are always forgiving and helping,*
*Even when we are yelling and yelping.*
*You are by far, the best mom,*
*In all ways, the perfect norm.*

*Your Silly Shanaya, who skipped the poetic gene'*

Karin entered her bedroom. The girls and Raoul had been playing board games. Three pairs of eyes looked at her with keen anticipation. She kissed each of them sentimentally and said with heartfelt sincerity, 'Thank you for a day that I will carry in my heart forever and ever after. I love you guys.'

They slept in one bedroom that night, just like old times, watching a rerun of *Dumb and Dumber*, playing Uno and singing songs on the karaoke machine. Karin stayed awake long after everyone fell asleep. She felt like she was soaking in a bathtub of bounty and wanted to luxuriate in the sensation at leisure. She had saved Raoul's last note for the end, as directed. Raoul's handwriting was precise and pointed, so much like him. Not a dash or a dot out of place. She sunk restfully into her pillow, angling herself to maximise the reading light.

*'My Dearest Darling Karin,*

*A poet I am not,*
*So what counts is the thought.*
*I take you for granted,*
*Fights, feuds, so many unwarranted.*
*Still to God, I always pray,*
*thanking Him for sending you my way.*
*You know I love you.*
*Holding this family together, you are the glue.*
*In this fleeting life,*
*You are my salvation, my wife.*
*Love, love and more love,*

*Raoul.*
*P.S. I know that poem sucked but it is my first fling at the poetry thing. The things I do for you! Thanks for always playing bad cop, absorbing the flak and making me look good.'*

Karin felt a feeling of warmth permeate through her, thinking of the effort it must have taken Raoul to write the poem. She fondled the veins of his hand. Karin skimmed the girls' hair which lay dishevelled on their faces in their sleep. Feeling complete and content in her recollections of the day gone by, she rested undisturbed, in the sanctuary of this rare unison. For once, no demons, no nightmares, and no Aksh.

# 17A

Karin,

All quiet in your quarter of the hood? The pressure is increasing and I have writer's block, the size of The Great Wall of China. I have been toying with the idea of writing specifically about a mother-son relationship since I have already delved into the universal family equation. I am sceptical about pulling it off convincingly but then desperate times call for desperate measures.

The foremost predicament I have to chew over is whether I want to continue to capitalise on a winning blueprint, the family dynamics that constituted my first novel. It does seem like I am limited in my repertoire. Would you want to read about my mother and me, as a reader? Or am I flogging a dead horse?

Though I do not profess to be an authority on the subject, the one thing I find interesting is the devotion and devotedness of the Indian mother to her son. He remains the apple of her eye, however rotten he may turn out to be. Deplorably, I plead guilty to taking mine for granted. I have never given a hoot about scratching below the surface. I am not too sure if I view my mother as anything more than a two-dimensional person.

A whiff of the theme and my mother will hound me into making this a rhapsodic tribute. I should write this, Bollywood style. The virtuous mother, the dutiful son. Jim, my agent, will be happy. My mother will be happy. I will be happy, having killed two birds with one stone.

The debate is, will I have killed my writing career in the process?

One-hit wonder?

Aksh

# 17B

Karin,

Awaiting your feedback on scaling The Great Wall of China. What's up? Long time no hear. You are usually Quick Gun Murugan in your replies. I hope the damsel is not in distress.

Aksh

# 18

# The Birthday Boy

There are birthday people. Those who love the presents, the merrymaking, the whole nine yards. Like Sia.

Then there are the non-birthday people. Those who hate the fuss and the forced gaiety that the occasion ushers. Like Aksh.

It was that time of the year again. Aksh knew his birthday celebrations were important to Sia so he tried to go along with her well-laid plans. Inwardly, his birthday discomposed Aksh but he had learned to choose his battles wisely. For the past few years, there was a set pattern to the day and Sia improvised around it.

1. Phone call at midnight on his birthday eve from his mother, who stayed up to wish him.
2. Breakfast in bed when he woke up. That was followed by what he believed was the jewel in the crown of the day. Sia in bed, wearing new lingerie, consenting enthusiastically to the sexual activity of his choice. This, for Aksh, was typically to lie back and enjoy it.
3. Birthday greetings from his father. Brusque and disinterested. Birthday greetings from Jim. Energetic and booming. Birthday greetings from Sia's folks. Polite and hurried.
4. Follow Sia's birthday timetable in out-and-out compliance, like a lamb to the slaughter, feigning *joie de vivre* for the remainder of the day.

5. Sia was never one to start his birthday with a bang and end it with a whimper. After an intimate dinner, the nightcap was wild sex before they passed out, drunk and spent.

6. Hangover introspection the morning after.

And so it continued year after year.

When Aksh Soni woke up, he was surprised to find Sia in her cotton kaftan, with the breakfast tray in hand.

'So why are we doing cute this year? Where have you hidden my naughty hottie or is there a striptease in the offing?' he asked hopefully.

'Happy Birthday, handsome!' She kissed him amorously. 'This year we break tradition. There is a big surprise in store for you.'

'What's wrong with tradition? I like tradition.' Aksh said as he tried to pull Sia into bed with him.

She disentangled herself from him. 'Aksh, don't spoil the surprise! Eat your breakfast!'

The breakfast tray had French toast, muffins, baked beans, a cheese cube, orange juice and a fortune cookie, flanking a suede jewellery box.

'Jewellery for me? Darling, you spoil me!' Aksh said mock seriously. 'Hmmm. Fortune cookie? Does Sia's crystal ball see an upward swing in my fortune?'

'You are a goof! Eat first, then open it. Save the fortune cookie for the last.' Sia's eyes were shining in excitement.

'Yes, boss!' said Aksh and gobbled up the breakfast. Sia watched him eat, smiling indulgently.

Aksh opened the jewellery box. There was a negative inside it. Holding it up to the light, he looked at it quizzically.

'What is this? The dirty picture?' Aksh stuck his tongue out.

'Open the cookie, Aksh!' Sia said impatiently.

Aksh split open the fortune cookie and took out the scroll of paper inside. Sia was watching his facial expressions keenly. Aksh Soni's cocky face turned pale as he read the scroll.

Those seven words which altered his life in a nanosecond.

*'You are going to be a father.'*

'I hope you are joking, Sia?' Aksh searched her face for an indicator but she looked stony faced.

'And that is your reaction? You know Aksh, I was praying that this would mean something to you, something that is as momentous as this. I am a fool!' Sia spat, incensed with him.

'Sia, listen to me, please. You dropped this on me, without warning. You caught me off guard. I have not even had a chance to sort out how I feel.' Aksh tried reasoning with her. He moved closer to her but she jumped off the bed, in utmost hostility.

'Let me tell you. You do not feel anything. I carry the load of all the feelings in this relationship. You are emotionally impotent, Aksh, even if you have proven your virility in other areas! I am not a convenience store which provides for your needs in bed and out of it. There is no return policy here!' Aksh had never seen Sia this furious.

'Sia, I am really sorry but you knew that about me. I am not good with commitment. A baby? Wow! That is a new level altogether. Fuck! This is coming out all wrong!'

Sia's shoulders had fallen in defeat. Her face was distorted with the effort of restraining her tears. Aksh leaned forward to hold her but she held her hand up to keep him at arm's length.

How blind had he been! How could he not have realised? This phase of sobriety, her indifference in the bedroom, that noticeable glow. The tell-tale signs of pregnancy were so clear in hindsight.

'We will deal with it, Sia, together. Give me time to process this. Please. Okay?'

'Suit yourself, Aksh. I have given you the best years of my life, what're a few days more? Happy Birthday, Aksh Soni. For a change, today is justifiably about you!'

Sia walked out of the bedroom, slamming the door shut behind her. Aksh tried to fathom his own feelings but it was all so tumultuous, that he could not think straight. Like an android, he wore his track pants and running shoes. Sia was in the living room, resting on the sofa. Her hand was across her eyes. Aksh kissed her forehead and mentioned to her that he was going for a run. A fact that was self-explanatory, given his sporty gear, but she did not glance at him or give the paltriest affirmation of having heard him.

Aksh ran past the cars, over the uneven road, mindlessly. His mind caught up with him soon enough. How could Sia dump this on him from nowhere and expect him to fall over himself? Her family would pounce on them to get married if they got to know of the baby. Could it even be called a baby at this point? Foetus. It sort of rhymed with coitus. Was that a coincidence? Semantics be damned! The bottom-line was that he was in a huge mess. He wanted to get on a train to nowhere. Anywhere but here. Could anyone outrun a train? Was there a way to measure the speed of a thought process versus the velocity of a train?

The faster Aksh ran, trying not to think, the more rapidly images began to spin in his head, like a carousel of confusion. His father, young and impressive in military gear. His mom looking lovely in a purple saree with blue paisleys. Sia, her curls flying, teasing him, ardour reflected in her eyes. Karin, waving her fingers at him, her rings shimmering. The images kept pirouetting, taking turns in the forefront. Aksh picked up more pace, trying to run straight as an arrow to stop the circular chain of thoughts in his mind. He was back in school on Sports Day. He, in his school uniform, running in a race, in lead position. His house captain, his housemates, all on their feet, cheering thunderously. The identical feeling of a parched throat, lungs ready to burst, stitches in the abdomen. The finish line seeming to race away from him as he got closer and his body arching, to touch that thin rope of victory. And then it all reached a head. A baby, its features, bulbous blobs of flesh, like the rest of its grotesque body. The carousel started grinding to a screeching halt. Aksh felt his legs buckling under him. He stopped and bent down, panting, his hands on his trembling knees. He was going to be a father. Or not. It all came down to that one crystallised protuberance of a heartbeat.

# 18A

Dear Karin,

Happy Birthday, Aksh. Thank you, Karin. How did you know? Oh yes, I forgot, I just mentioned it.

On this sterling day, let me give you some Aksh Soni trivia. My name, the meaning of which, I have explained to many a reader, as you are well aware and have insolently exploited earlier, means axis. My name, given to me by my parents, is actually an abridged rendition of my father's name. The chariot of a thousand horses, that is the meaning of my name, the one of my choosing. Imagine the beauty of a thousand horses, with thundering hooves, running in one fluid motion. What if any one horse chose to pull away? Would he be herded back in, trampled by his compatriot equines for his insurgency? Then there would be 999. The chariot with 999 horses. It definitely does not have power of a thousand. That one deviant horse was what made them a formidable force of four figures.

From numbers to alphabets. You know that alphabet game? I am going to use it to describe this day of celebration.

A for apocalypse

B for baby

C for commitment

D for dismay and so on forth.

Sia is pregnant. Congratulations. Thank you. After me, you are the first to know. That was my birthday gift from her. This prize of progeny. She might as well have put a shotgun to my head. I handled the glad tidings with as much sangfroid as handling a blistering, hot potato. Have I ever told you I am an asshole, if you have not figured that out already? Self-admittedly, I have hurt her many a time and swept it under the rug of relationships. This hurt was different. When she broke the news to me, that needy expectancy in her eyes, it evoked a flight response. I fled. She bled. Is this relationship henceforward dead?

Any advice on how to reform an asshole? Woman to man.

The not-so-happy birthday boy,

Aksh

P.S. Hey Pacemaker, I need you to ring the starting bell and you do the disappearing act? The mother-son narrative awaits your verdict.

# 18B

Dear Aksh,

I am going to let you read an excerpt from my private diary. Your birthday present. Happy Birthday, Aksh.

*There are many vindictive missiles a couple launches to attack each other in marital space. But the single meanest thing Raoul has ever said, and mind you this is to prove his point in an argument: What if I think you dance too wildly? What if I do not like the way you dance at all? This is after a decade together. After the ironical fact that we met at a night club. That he watched me dance and then came up to me. That what distinguishes us as a couple is, we love to dance, impervious to the world. That is what broke my heart. Dancing is the support that steadied me on the precipice of sanity. A bad grade, a fight with my parents, stressed with the kids. Music is that fabric which screened me seamlessly through the years. Given that I could dance, I knew I would see that day through, that moment through. So understand why a part of me died, why my feet will seem more leaden, why my abandon will be plagued with caution. I suspect the music will remain a hum from a bygone time. My feet will tap. My heart will dance. I will want to move till the music fills the lacuna within. But the music died today as his callousness torched my rope of redemption. And he knows not what he killed.*

This was written around ten years ago. Couples fight. They survive. We did. Yes, I still dance. Alone. And also together. Marriage, motherhood, fatherhood, they are all myths that transform us into aspiring legends. The best wife in the world. The best father or mother in the world. We aspire to be like the greeting cards that we receive. That is the hallmark (my turn to be 'punny'). Marital bliss is a masochistic misnomer. The only time a couple can be in that exalted state, is when they are enshrined in adjoining graves. Having said that, here is the plus side. Without someone by your side, the days would be dull and drab, the nights would be destitute and dismal. We need connection. Connection comes at a cost. Freedom in reciprocity for constancy. Why marry or have kids then, is what must have crossed your mind. Be it four stages of life in the ancient Hindu scriptures or the seven ages of Shakespeare's man, they tout a natural progression of life. Passion can be bought for a price from a street corner, but sharing the journey of life with another human being is an entitlement. So after the passion is spent over the years, and the partying slowly ends, what's left? The companionship remains. The children evolve, branch out and that tree of life sustains you with its life force. Commitment is life altering and once in a while, life threatening too! There are days I could kill someone and the shackles bite into my runaway ankles. Then there are many more days where the anchor of Raoul and the girls, keeps me buoyant. Looking back, I would not have it any other way.

Aksh, you can choose to swim against the tide. That choice is yours. The fact that you have been in a long-term relationship, is evidence enough that you need someone. As a woman, I know Sia will take time to forgive you. Mend fences before they cave in. As for fatherhood, it will bathe you with indescribable feelings. That podgy baby finger curling around your own arouses such protectiveness, such love, like you have never known it.

Even if your chariot has a thousand horses, the direction can only be one.

Your agony aunt,

Karin

P.S. Sorry about the delay. I would love to read about the mother and son relationship but only if you can pull it off, like you did so ingeniously in your previous book. You need to have conviction, Aksh. Your fans, yours truly included, deserve your optimum output. Do not sell yourself short.

# 18C

Karin,

'There was once a little boy. A good, little boy. His childhood was happy besides the nicks and cuts of growing up. He wanted to be a soldier, just like his dad. He was eleven when his father was sent back from the war, injured and retired from duty. After that he failed at every duty, be it father or husband. His father's amputated leg made its concealed occupancy felt all over the boy's life. In the nights, when he could hear his mother subduing her sobs, as she stood at the gunpoint of her husband's frustrated rage. In the day, when the boy tiptoed around the house, avoiding the man that bore the face of his father, but none of his earlier personality.

He cried in his mother's arms.

"Why why does he not play with me anymore?"

"Why why does he get angry at you?"

"Why why does he not love us?"

She held him close and replied gently.

"He is not angry at you or me. He is angry at himself. He loves us but has forgotten how to show it. His heart is damaged and needs to heal. Be patient. Till then you have to be a big, brave boy and make him proud."

The boy took his mother's advice to heart and resolved to win back his father. He studied and topped his class. He never demanded anything. He did not watch too much television. He had no close friends. So he read and read, and filled the hollow void with imaginary worlds. He waited. The time never came. The father he knew, lay entombed in the sarcophagus of this stranger he called Dad.

*Unhurriedly the lesions healed and Dad returned, not fully, still half a man. Dad tried to reach out but it was too late. He had lost his son to the war he had brought home. In high school, the boy decided to become a writer. His father fought him fiercely as if he was back in the combat zone. The boy fought back. He fought back because this was one dream that nobody was going to pillage from him. It was then that the boy amputated himself from emotion, from sworn duty. He had grown up to be exactly like his father.'*

Me

# 18D

Dearest Aksh,

I get it now.

I am sorry.

For you.

For me.

I know the excreta of our pasts is strewn over the sands of time and we are enshrouded beneath its gritty layers. No pricey perfume that Raoul buys can mask its putrid pungency. No sweet caress of Sia's can wash away the filth. Destiny used her ruthless chisel and hacked away at our bedrock, till our hearts have almost turned to stone. The pain of being hurt is like a scorching, intense fire. It can leave your heart, blackened and bitter or it can purify and turn it into gold. That is the mettle of a person and only after conquering extreme adversity, will the true substance be detected. It seems the element of one's aura is unearthed only after it passes the litmus test of hardship. We are undeniably contaminated characters. Nevertheless, the power to pen the remaining chapters is yours, at long last. Wield it as you must.

Hugs,

Karin

# 19

## Flurry

Flurry Mehra was the most loved member of the family. The offshoot of a blitz of wrangling and imploring, raging through the portals of the Mehra home for many weeks.

What happens when we travel?

The maids or a friend will handle him.

Who will take care of him daily?

We will. That is the point. We will learn to be more responsible.

You know how tough it will be when he dies?

We all know we are going to die anyway so does that mean we do not live?

It was Amara's metaphysical point that clinched the conflict and it was game, set and match.

After much negotiation, the warring factions of parents versus children, came to an amicable compromise. No dog. No cat. A rabbit.

Astonishingly, Raoul, the most vehement advocate of a pet-free home, had developed a fondness for the grey and white fur ball with lamblike eyes. Raoul would act nonchalant but Flurry and he had a mutual admiration society, doubtlessly due to the treats Raoul fed him on the sly. Karin and the girls would tease Raoul about his initial reservations, but he would always deny his abiding attachment to the animal. Flurry would hop all over the room which was allocated to him. He was an alert and responsive animal and his long ears would wiggle at the sound of his name. The wily rabbit that he was, he managed to hop his way into the hearts of all members of the Mehra household. Raoul and Karin had to grudgingly admit aloud that the rabbit had a therapeutic influence on the family, particularly the girls.

The girls used to celebrate his birthday, strewing the room with sprigs of coriander and grated carrots. They would cut a cake, holding his paw, even managing to make him wear a party hat and pose for selfies. It was around a week after his second birthday, that Flurry seemed under the weather. Karin noticed his droppings were liquefied and his movements lethargic. He was not eating anything including his beloved treats. The girls were not at home and Raoul came back from the office on Karin's behest. Their regular vet was unaccustomed to the treatment of a critically ill rabbit, hence he suggested another vet in the suburbs. Flurry lay lolling in the crook of Karin's arm through the unending drive. Raoul was getting increasingly crabby with the driver and the traffic. To add to their problems, the vet was unavailable when they arrived. After persistent enquiries, Raoul found out that he stayed in the vicinity and managed to convince him about the emergency of the case. The vet lay Flurry on the examining table and decided to inject him with fast acting antibiotics gauging his deteriorating condition. As soon as the needle perforated Flurry's thin skin, a high-pitched, blood-curdling shriek emanated from the poor animal. Raoul and Karin were stunned at the hair-raising and siren-like sound of torment from the hitherto speechless creature. It sent a chill down Karin's spine and she jittered involuntarily.

'Are you sure he will be fine, Doctor? What is your diagnosis?' Raoul's concern was evident in his brisk queries.

'I think he has an amoebic infection. Bring him back tomorrow so I can give him another dose of antibiotics,' suggested the vet.

On the drive back, Flurry was lying supine on Karin's lap and then all of a sudden, his body started lurching and then went into unmanageable spasms. Raoul and she held Flurry down, but his body would not stop writhing. They were petrified and desperation was mirrored in the other's eyes. It went on like this for an indeterminate period of time. Then it was over, almost like he had snapped. Flurry was motionless, his eyes glassy with the stare of death and his body rigid as a board, fully outstretched. Karin's tears fell on the matted fur of the still creature and she felt the dampness with trepidation. Her eyes were glued on the road loping ahead as her hands groomed the fur, in a pointless pursuit to disentangle it. Raoul moved her hand and held it in his own, without looking at her. His other hand rested on Flurry's lifeless body all the way home.

'Oh God, Raoul. I cannot tell the kids. It will break their hearts. I will not be able to handle it.' Karin cried.

'I will take care of it, Karin. Thank goodness his pain was not prolonged.' Raoul consoled her.

Karin waited for the girls to return from college. Neither Raoul nor she wanted to eat a nibble. Even the staff was distraught with the loss. The ache was gnawing and growing, chomping its way through the whole house.

The door bell rang and both girls dashed into the bedroom after a few minutes.

'Where is Flurry? How come Papa is home?' Shanaya asked, puzzled.

'Sit down, girls,' Raoul said gently.

'What happened, Papa?' Amara was terror stricken.

'Flurry was ill in the morning so we took him to the vet. I am so sorry but we could not manage to save him.'

'He...he died? Flurry died?' Shanaya started blubbering.

Karin enfolded Shanaya in her arms as heartbreak racked her willowy body. She tried to draw Amara close too but her move was met with resistance.

'Where is he, Papa?' Amara's voice was fearful.

Raoul's shoulders seemed to cave in as he pointed to the sheet covered bulge on the floor.

'How can you keep him on the floor? Why can't you keep him in his room? What if he smells his food and it wakes him up? How can you be so mean?' Amara was berserk with bereavement.

Her hands were shaking as she opened the carefully swaddled carcass of the rabbit. And then she broke down. The face of death was unambiguous and irrevocable.

'Cry, baby, cry it out. He was taken away very gently while he was lying in Mamma's lap.' Raoul held Amara close to his chest.

'Papa, why does he look like he is smiling? Are you sure he is dead?' Shanaya asked hesitantly.

'He lived a very happy life because of the love you girls gave him, that's why he was able to leave with a smile. Mamma and I loved him too, you know that,' Raoul said softly.

All four of them wrote messages and prayers for Flurry. They enwrapped him in handcrafted paper along with the penned epitaphs. Then Raoul drove them to the waterfront promenade, where they laid him to rest in the sea.

Karin and Raoul put Amara and Shanaya to bed, like they used to, when the girls were small. Karin sang lullabies to them, which sent them into fits of giggling interspersed with bouts of sobbing. Flanked by their parents, exhausted with weeping, the girls dozed off. Only then did Karin and Raoul leave their side.

'Thank you, Raoul, for taking care of things,' Karin said as Raoul followed her into bed, a few minutes later.

'Thank you, Karin, for my girls and for our home.'

His voice was teeming with emotion. Karin felt a lump rising to her throat and lodging itself there. She touched Raoul's fingertips to her mouth and realised they smelled of coriander and rabbit treats.

# 19A

Dear Aksh,

I cannot sleep. Did I mention we have a rabbit? Amendment. We had a rabbit. He died this morning. Flurry was his name. I never realised how much Flurry united our family, more than ever, in his demise. It was like a holy nexus, a communion of grief. The grief, Aksh, is like splinters of memories, impaling my entire being. Does it sound over the top? This extreme feeling for a rabbit? I ask myself that too.

We speak of unconditional love as if there is such a thing. Not between humans in my opinion, but certainly in the love between man and the beast he nurtures. What can one expect from an animal? His need for you, his lack of inhibition, it makes for the most uncomplicated oneness. Perhaps it sounds amplified but this feels like a free fall and the dejection is gradually sinking in. Flurry's warm body turned cold in the cradle of my limbs and I could do nothing but watch his life ebb away, in a series of dying breaths.

Karin

# 19B

Dear Karin,

R.I.P. Flurry.

I had two turtles once. It was all we could afford. Kiara and Kovu. I loved *The Lion King* series. They lived in a small tub in our shabby balcony. They were black turtles and I used to believe that they were sent from heaven, specially for me. I never knew if they were really of different genders but Kiara's markings were vague while Kovu had more pronounced flecks on his shell. They were like sumo wrestlers lumbering along with their stubby legs. It was something to look forward to when I got home from school. They would respond to the sound of my voice, craning their necks to the utmost. They would nip my finger when I fed them, razor-sharp kisses, I used to think. They had eyes like wise old men and I would narrate my stories to them. It sounds childish now but I believed they actually understood what I was saying. If they waddled off mid sentence, I would tear up the story and rewrite it. They were both, my sounding boards and first critics. I know that sounds plaintive and absurd.

What I enjoyed most was scrubbing their dome-shaped flinty backs with a soft, used toothbrush. My least favourite was when the water would turn smelly and I would have to wash their tub spotlessly clean. While I did that, they would run as fast as their scaly legs would carry them, which was never too far, considering the size of our home.

It was a day like any other and when I got back from school, they were waiting, their necks craning. As I went down on my knees to pet their leathery napes, I almost threw up. Both Kiara and Kovu had their eyes gouged out and their V-shaped mouths were open, as if paralysed in a countenance of horror. The rats had mutilated them, after mauling them to death. I had overlooked placing the cover on their tub. It was due to my negligence that those murderous rodents had snuffed out the lives of my turtles, in the most gruesome manner imaginable. That horrific image will stay with me till the end of my days.

I did not speak to anyone. I cried at nights, alone. It would have been awkward to express. I was a boy after all.

The grief is completely justified.

I understand.

Cry. I am here.

Aksh

# 20

# Patrimony

One of the things that drew Aksh to Sia was her stoic disposition. She took things in her stride and handled them with a pinch of salt. However, since the baby blowout, she seemed to have changed. She was not aggressive by nature, but there was an uneasy ceasefire enveloping their relationship. Aksh realised it was more destructive than any violent tempest. The conversation was functional, the answers monosyllabic. Worst of all, Sia had lost the twinkle in her eyes. They lay on the same bed, ate on the same table, but moved on adjacent tracks.

It was almost a week since his birthday fiasco. Time had flown and frozen, both at once. The baby was an actuality reinforced by Sia's careful movements, the pillow between them at nights, and by the absence of any real communication.

Television had become Aksh's new best friend. Over the din of audio-visual mayhem, he heard his phone vibrate. In no mood for small talk with his mother, he turned a deaf ear to the call. Sia was preparing a meal in the kitchen so he was spared the moral lecture. The door almost fell of its rusty hinges, as an overwrought Sia rushed into the bedroom.

'Aksh! It's your dad. He had a fall! Your mom found him unconscious in the bathroom. She called for an ambulance and has taken him to the hospital,' Sia shouted.

'Your mom has been calling. Why didn't you answer your phone?'

Aksh bolted from the bed.

'Goddamn it! How was I to know she was calling for this? Which hospital?'

Bit-by-bit the feelings were sinking in and nose-diving into the bottomless pit of his stomach.

By the time he got in touch with his hysterical mother, Sia was already at the door, handbag and car keys in hand.

Sia drove to the hospital. She touched Aksh's elbow, gingerly.

'He will be fine. He is a tough cookie,' she offered.

Aksh's face was impassive and unmoving.

They walked by the full-sized Ganesha idol in the main lobby. The receptacle for so many prayers and pleas could not have found a better platform, than in the innards of illness and death. The antiseptic smell of the hospital assaulted their senses. Sia thought she was going to swoon but took a few deep breaths and managed to compose herself. The elevator ride to the I.C.U. was a series of disagreeable vignettes of wheelchairs and stretchers.

Reena Soni held out her arms to her only child when she saw him. Her body heaved and crumpled as Aksh held his mother. His father had had a fall in the bathroom. The doctors said there seemed to be a clot. The results would be confirmed after further tests.

'He kept it from us. He had been feeling numbness and hand tremors but you know how he is. Go to him. He has been asking for you.' His mother spoke in a hushed tone, as if her voice would make its way past the swinging doors of the Neurology ward. The apprehension of seeing him in that condition made Aksh cringe. It made his blood boil as to how his father could arbitrarily choose to keep them in ignorance? How many times were they pressurised to cope with the protracted purgatory of thinking he was dead or dying? Aksh was decidedly angry. It was a lot better than fear. In one fell swoop, his father had catapulted him back into those boyhood days of insecurity. Dad. He recapitulated the word in his head a few times, but it sounded invented and disconnected.

Through the protective barrier of the glass, he saw his father. Akshay's caliper was upstanding in the corner, like a sentinel, safeguarding the room. Aksh could see the shape of his stump under the blanket and the shrapnel of adolescence pricked him. He had come back from school. The heat was sweltering. His father had dozed off and the coverlet had slipped off his body. Aksh remembered being both mesmerised and repulsed, at the sight of what had once been a leg. A leg, that Aksh had gambolled on many a joyride. A fly was hovering around the scabs and festering incisions, inflicted by the continuous grazing of the caliper. Its senses reeling, it whirled like a dervish, enraptured by the decay of the raw stub of tissue and bone. It seemed to have travelled through time and possessed his father's body. The monitors were attached to him, like a web, and he looked like a fly, enmeshed in the midst of all the wires.

Aksh was ambushed by a battalion of feelings and memories. They came at him, like his night terrors of headless horsemen riding on phantom horses through the mists of times. His childhood collection of cardboard boxes, each one painted painstakingly with a religious symbol from all faiths. Back then, he used to pray daily in the hope that if he prayed rigorously enough he could harness his father's voice, his snoring, his sum and substance, in those magical boxes. In case, his father did not return from the war, the boy could hold on to him through them. That paper boat of pipe dreams sailed around lopsidedly, in view again.

'Dad?' Aksh addressed him in a muted tone.

Akshay Soni's eyes opened, even before the word fully left his son's mouth. His cadaverous eyes smiled and the debilitation in them was unbearable for Aksh. His father held out his hand and Aksh was baffled for a minute. He dithered, before he finally rested his own hand in his father's. They stayed that way for a few seconds, avoiding any other communication. Aksh felt acute uneasiness at this atypical situation.

'Rest, Dad. I will take care of things. Don't worry.' Aksh reassured him and left the room, walking backwards. His father's eyes did not leave him. Aksh squirreled away his sentiments before he went out to his mother and Sia.

Sia was sitting in silent camaraderie beside his mom. His mother looked beaten. Her body language was unrecognisable to him. He was used to seeing her positive and optimistic, through all the ups and downs of life. The half-full glass seemed to have emptied itself on Reena Soni. She looked old and fatigued as she gave him a weak smile. He wanted to hug her tight, real tight. He wanted to apologise on behalf of his father. He wanted to apologise for his own behaviour and tell her he loved her. Overriding all of that, he wanted to run far away from all of them, as far as possible.

Aksh Soni had no capacity to deal with losing his father again. He had been nailed to that crucible enough. He had no strength to take care of his mother, if and when his father was no more. That situation seemed to be imminent in the near future, death projecting its presence, as large as life. As much as he resented his father and got snappy with his mother, the very idea of their perpetual absence was frightening. He would discontinue to be somebody's son. He never even had a full chance to be a child. It was bloody unfair. The unconstrained buffer that a parent provides, that he took for granted, it was all to be gone. If not today, then tomorrow. One parent was on a downward descent, one to go. And then there were Sia and the baby. Aksh felt a sense of impending doom. The chickens had come home to roost. Sooner or later, he had to take care of the coop.

His entire world was topsy turvy. The events of the past few days had taken enough of a toll on him. First, the baby and now this! Right now, he needed to detach from all of them and their oppressive need of him or he would go crazy. The only thing that seemed to matter was a double shot of espresso macchiato. And Karin.

# 20A

Dear Karin,

*'Once upon a time, there was a little boy. Once upon a time, there was a little girl. They lived in divergent worlds but spoke the same language. Destiny forcefully intervened and their paths converged in quick succession. On the face of it, they had nothing in common except an indelible, insidious past. But then that was everything.*

*The wailing wind carried their secrets to and fro. The starless nights cloaked their tribulation from the prying eyes of dawn. It was only the tales they shared, that carried them through the long, lonely days. Their ending may not be a happy one because that happens only in fiction. The thing with being so broken was that nobody could take either of them apart again or make them whole again. Each maimed piece would rise in dissent. Eventually, they found in each other, the alloy, to weld their wounds into a semblance of cohesion. Their ending may, in due course, be a peaceful one.'*

Meet me, Karin. Let's break down this barricade of words and find what we might be together.

Aksh

# 21

## Uncleji

'Karin! How much longer are you going to take? This is ridiculous, even for you! It is *your* uncle's birthday, not my uncle's! Your folks have called twice. Karin!' Raoul pummelled his fists at the bathroom door.

'Raoul, go and nag the girls to get ready. I will be done before them.' Karin answered as normally as she could muster.

Nothing about Karin was normal. She was sitting on the floor of the bathroom, the shower running above and her head bent down on her knees. Karin rocked. The globules of water scurried out of her way. It had been years since she had seen her uncle. To go partake in the celebration of his eightieth birthday, wish him, perhaps even hug him, made her nauseous. Maybe if she sat under the shower longer, she would catch a chill, followed by a fever and then she would have a satisfactory pretext to stay home. She could hear Raoul yelling at the girls to hurry. She hauled herself off the floor. The mirror had condensed and she wiped it, wondering how simple life would be if one could just wipe out the past with a swipe. She wiped the mirror again. And again. As she dried her hair, she fantasised about slapping her uncle, one hefty slap across his face. Happy Birthday, Uncleji, I wish you were never born actually. The idea gave her an iota of comfort. She had only seen him in passing a few years ago.

From the time her family had sold their sprawling Teen Batti bungalow to go their separate ways, she had rarely met him. Age had cut him down to size and he was as slender as a reed. Who would have thought this harmless looking, god-fearing man was capable of such atrocity? Karin's hands shook as she applied her makeup. She was a forty-six-year-old woman who could easily break the old man's bones if she squeezed his hand a bit too firmly. She should do that. Look him straight in the eye, crush his bones, each finger, one at a time. When he would cry out in agony, she would ask him if he wanted a special lollipop. Karin knew her uncle would never meet her gaze again. He just wanted to slink away to Hell, leaving her with his cross to bear.

'You okay? You look flushed.' Raoul touched her forehead.

'Yes, I'm good. It's nothing. Thanks. I had a really hot shower, perhaps that's why,' Karin replied.

'We better get going, Karin. Don't forget the gift.' Raoul sprayed on his cologne.

Amara and Shanaya entered the room, dressed and sullen, their usual counter to Raoul's disgruntlement at their tardiness.

'My two princesses and my queen are looking gorgeous. I am going to be a very envied man tonight.' He patted the girls' heads. They melted and started chattering away all the way from the house to the car. Karin, like most women, was a master at multitasking. She responded, laughed and even managed to throw in a joke, while her mind was plaiting itself into stiff knots of stress.

As they entered the party hall, her heart rate was accelerating, intimating the launch of a panic attack. The hall was dressed very spartan, probably keeping in mind Chachaji's simplicity of character. Except for candlelit bowls of yellowing white jasmine flowers floating in water on the tables, there were no extra frills. The sickly fragrance besieged her anxious mind even further. Most of the family was thronging around the centre of the area. The melee of people seemed to fall like nine pins as she saw the wizened birthday boy. In his white muslin clothes, he looked like a guru surrounded by his coterie of followers. It felt like the parting of the Red Sea as her legs, in revolt, straggled along the stretch of bruised carpet. She wanted to run back but her parents were waving at her from afar as they stood beside Uncleji. *Her* parents. She had sheltered them, so they retained their blissful innocence even if she had lost hers in the bargain. That guileless brain intuitively knew, even back then, that devastation would prevail along with the truth. She made the choice to slit her psyche so that they could survive but now she was consumed with a fanatic urge to crush their impression of the illustrious Uncleji. 'This too shall pass,' she kept chanting in her head.

Raoul bent down to touch the feet of the seniors. Uncleji patted him on the head. He then turned to the girls who bent down to wish him. Karin wanted to yank them away from his grasp. His fingers looked like pincers, browning and shivering with the vagaries of old age. Each wave of nausea passing through her was stronger than the other. She went forward in a zombie-like state and murmured something meant to be congratulatory. Everyone was watching. Her mind continued goading her to strip him down to the naked truth in front of all his loved ones. Uncle's eyes met hers and darted away instantaneously. *The miserable paedophile. A puny bag of bones. An unequal opponent.* Then the feeling faded. What purpose was it going to serve? The affliction of his misdoings was his to carry to the grave. And hers.

Along with the pleats of her saree, she gathered herself and sat at the far end of the table. Uncle was in her peripheral vision so she changed her placement to block him out.

'Hey babe. Feeling better? Can I get you a drink?' Raoul came over to her.

'Yes, I am. A glass of champagne is what the doctor prescribed. Thanks,' Karin replied.

'Look at your rockstar uncle, Karin! He is breaking out into a jig! What a dude!' Karin had no choice but to turn her head towards the action.

Uncleji was dancing timidly, clutching the hands of his simpering wife. Everyone was encouraging them vociferously. Again the fury resurfaced and Karin wanted to take a stick and break those spindly legs that had pinned her down with such brute force. The family joined in and Karin was forced to go on the floor upon Raoul's insistence. Uncleji looked directly at her, bent his head and joined his hands together, in what others may have witnessed as an indication of thanks. Alarmed and astonished at this brazenness, only Karin knew that this was his apology, almost four decades later. Too little, too late. The slate was too smudged to be wiped clean.

The rest of the night passed in a blur of family anecdotes. For all the grumbling about boring family get-togethers, the girls seemed to be enjoying the attention and warmth showered on them. Karin felt a fierce surge of love and protection towards them. She revelled in their girlish giggles, untainted by any reprehensible history. Amara's abundant eyelashes, so much like her father's and

Shanaya's chasmic dimples, so much like her own. The alchemy of both their genes was fascinating. She watched Raoul help her mom rise from the chair and then get her dad a drink. Raoul had grown to be a son to her family, always gallant and solicitous. Their life together flashed before her eyes, causing them to mist over in memory. He was a good man. A time-tested, known man.

The drive back home was full of stories and mirthful laughter about the people at the party. The weirdest person award, declared by Raoul, went to Karin's maternal cousin and his wife who insisted on a romantic Marco Polo game in public. If he called her sweetie, she called him pie, if she called him baby, he called her doll. The special mention award went to her aunt who faked interest in listening and asked the girls thrice in the same evening what they were studying. Oblivious to Karin's lack of participation, they prattled on, making her feel alienated. She, without exception, felt this way in this family of her own choice and making. Later, as Raoul lay in bed watching her apply her night cream, she glanced at him through the mirror.

'Why so serious?' He pulled his Joker face from his favourite *Batman* film.

'Raoul, I want to talk to you about something.' Karin had no idea why that fugitive utterance broke through.

'Uh oh. Now what did I do wrong?' Raoul bantered.

'Just hold me, Raoul, please. And listen, just listen.' Karin curled up against him.

Each singeing tear she shed, exorcised the demons of her past, leaving them crucified and defenceless. She told him everything, every sordid detail, from childhood to the Karin of now, while nervously playing with the hair on her husband's chest, anointing him with a lifetime of her pain. This time, Karin held nothing back. Except about Aksh Soni. She had to make her own way across that precarious terrain.

'Karin, I am so sorry. Twenty-three years and you have been carrying this inside you. Did you not trust me to love you? I would have broken that bastard's bones if I had known earlier! I cannot believe I was forcing you to dance with him. The thought makes me want to punch myself! Why did you not tell me, Karin?' Raoul questioned.

'What does one do when you spend half your life dreaming of someone like you and when he is ultimately yours, you spend the rest of your life too afraid to believe, wondering if and when it will end and whether he really is yours or ever can be? Are all dreams just sugar-coated nightmares? How do you explain to someone that you love him so much, that actually believing that he loves you as much, frightens you, because you know if that belief is destroyed, if there is even a little crack in that gleaming facade, you will collapse irretrievably into tiny, irreparable pieces?

How do you tell that man that each time you take a glimpse into your bedroom, a part of you lies in bed with him, steeling yourself in anticipation of his touch, because another part stands peeking through the door, afraid to fully enter inside, to fully share that world?

How do you tell someone that you love him so much, it is beyond age, looks and intellect? A sublime love that is deformed by insecurity and fear. All you would want to do, is to scream, "if you loved me as much as I loved you, if only I knew, if only I believed."

Karin wiped her tear-smudged face with the back of her hand as she paused for breath.

'Raoul, I never trusted that you could love me if you knew the truth. My mind is like a toilet bowl of fetid memories. I was afraid that unclogging it would flush away my life with you. Today, my mind came to a drastic revelation. Uncleji has robbed me of an entire childhood but it is I, who has allowed him to rob me of a lifetime of feeling. I have never let the girls or you breach the walls that I built. A part of me has always been imprisoned in that room, chained to that shame. It will probably always stay there, along with the childhood I lost. I hope you understand.'

Karin hesitated for a moment and then taking a deep breath, she started playing with the edge of the pillow cover as she continued talking.

'It does not help that I am getting older too. I look it and feel it. It's like I am withering away. Each part of me is drying up and getting uglier as I age. Why would you want me? What if you leave? I am petrified to fully love you. I am terrified to trust in permanence. For withholding all of me from you, I am genuinely sorry. I am tired, Raoul, of this alienation, of this emptiness.'

'You were never alone. I am here, Karin. I was always here, if you had looked closely. And I will always want you. I'd be lost without you. Those lines on your face not only add character to your beauty but chart the life we have shared. Besides, you know, I have a thing for older women. But jokes aside, doesn't the true beauty lie in the fact that we are growing old together, that we are lucky enough to have each other when we need love or reassurance? That itself defeats time. I am going nowhere. I will never let anyone hurt you. I will protect you and the girls, for as long as I live. You don't have to be afraid ever again. I promise. . . .'

Karin had read many a famed poet and philosopher, fascinated with their prowess, but none had moved her as much as the simplicity of Raoul's promise.

She turned off the lights and nestled against him. The dark did not seem so terrifying. Raoul caressed her face, and for the first time in their marriage, Karin did not flinch from the palliative tenderness of his touch.

# 21A

Dearest Aksh,

There are these tufts of nothingness that glide through the air, their diaphanous bodies cocooning the sunlight. They pass by. I have always wanted to touch them, hold them and discover the ethos of their free spirit. Yet I know instinctively, I must not. Wispy, fragile and undefinable. Like these feelings.

Aksh, love as it is supposed to be, is what you have with Sia and I have with Raoul. With them, we have history which can never repeat or be rewritten. It is the indiscernible fulcrum that grounds us while we turn labyrinthine cartwheels in these loops of loneliness. What you and I have, is a thing apart. An affinity of almost celestial proportion, and for all that, it is but an illusion.

If we let fallibility tarnish it, it becomes banal. But banality is what life is about. This realm you and I share, where our souls and feelings dance in such splendid synchrony, is beyond and above a tangible meaning.

You do know deep down in your heart, that this is beautiful only because it is unattainable. We are perfect, only on paper. That sacrosanct blankness that grips our minds in its alluring tentacles of promise. You have love in your life but you do not let it wash over you and soothe you. Neither have I. We are desolate, smouldering, and most of all, we are afraid.

We spent our lives searching for a kindred spirit and when we met, the relatedness egged us into dimensions that seemed to fill the vacuum in both of us. We are like stunted saplings who have forgotten that seasons change. In order to endure our wintry past, we grew these brambles. It is time to succumb to the summer of the present. It is time to bloom to the emotional heights we were destined to soar. It is time to let go of each other, and realise it is only our words that made love to each other, thrashing around on a bed traumatised by thorns.

Whether it is being a father to my girls, like when Flurry passed away. Or being a son to my parents whenever they need him. Or trying his best as a husband, to bring a smile to my face. It has taken Raoul over two decades to build these bridges. I cannot burn them for the compelling impulse to explore the what-if of this make-believe world that you and I have fabricated.

Reality is my daughter jabbering about her latest theatrical fight with her friends. Reality is Sia and your mother cajoling you into wearing a suit. Reality is Raoul's ritual of fastening the lock of my bracelet. Reality is your unborn child. Reality is the realisation that my feelings for Raoul transcend this abyss within me.

There is incomparable succour in the inanity.

You and I. We will consume each other.

Like we do those who love us, despite us.

That is who we are.

Aksh, you have it all. Breathe your lifeblood into the translucence. Let go. Love. Love fearlessly. The way you write. Exactly the way you write. Dive in and claim the life that is waiting for you.

Someday, I hope to meet you on that marquee. My tale has always taken a backseat to love, to obligation. Maybe forever. How intolerable is that? I will suffuse my being with the gratitude of my life. Who knows, maybe one day my story will emerge, unfettered.

Aksh. Aksh. Aksh.

Your name will unceasingly rustle in my head.

And it will complete itself into an Akshar, the exquisite word, like no other, existing wholly in its entirety.

That will be the beginning of my journey.

But this is the end of ours.

I will not say something as trivial as goodbye because I am bound to you by every memory, every thought, in a secluded glen of solitude, that belongs only to us.

I am bound to you till the words cease, and echo on beyond eternity.

Always,

Karin

# 22

# The Purge

Aksh felt an out-and-out dread. It had been an alien feeling for a while. Yet it was so customary in the cavities of time, dead and buried. That rumbling tummy before an exam. That clump of foreboding before an interview. He propped the pillows and shifted into a raised posture, adroitly evading Sia's sleeping form. The guilt of his surreptitiousness added to the contortions of turmoil in his intestines. The only thing he had ever offered Sia in totality was fidelity, and finding out about Karin and him would break her, even though nothing had happened so far. Not in any real sense.

Technology's single click and there was Karin. Live, breathing and enveloped in the white light of the screen. His eyes scoured the page, registering nothing. He slapped his face lightly, to slow down the pounding in his heart. The reverberations seemed so audible, he hyperventilated, thinking Sia could hear them. He wanted to retch and dousing the acridity in his mouth, he focussed his eyes on the screen again.

He knew he had lost her even before he had finished reading the mail. That infuriating, kooky, unpredictable woman! He was going to give her a piece of his mind. She could not traipse in and out of his life as she pleased. He pressed the reply key but he could think of nothing to write. He just stared. And then the epiphany hit him hard. Need. He needed her. At the beck and call of his convoluted mind. A renegade emotion that defied all logic. She was the figment of imagination that he had created, craved, because real life extracted such a pound of flesh. He needed her, to forget about all else.

At first, he thought it was the harsh whiteness of the screen that was blurring his eyes. Then there was this compression in his throat. He tried to swallow and suddenly his face was hot and flushed. The last time Aksh had cried, was when he was sixteen and his grandmother had died. The tears were rolling down his cheeks, leaving him bewildered. They seemed to have a mind of their own, hurtling down his face, incensing him. The more enraged he was, the more defiantly they tumbled down. Aksh Soni had no idea why he was crying. Or when the crying turned into sobbing. His body shook, convulsing and disembodied, the remorse took wings and bellowed its conquest.

'Aksh! Aksh! What happened? Are you crying? Aksh! Is everything okay?'

Sia had snapped out of her sleep, shocked at the sight of Aksh.

'Sia. I am sorry, for everything. I cannot run anymore. I need a place to rest. These words, they act like they befriend you but then they backstab you, leaving you so lonely. And still you keep hunting for I do not know what. And then before you know it, all you have are your paperbacks and hardbacks, disintegrating on dusty shelves. Shelves that nobody has cleaned because there is nobody to pick up after you. The realisation knocks you over, that the words are vacuous, plain verbosity, enticing you with the misleading vision of a better existence. They have incarcerated you along with themselves in a life sentence. A malignant curse they are, these words. Do you understand, Sia? Even I don't understand a bloody word of what I am saying! I don't even know why you would want to be with a selfish prick like me. I can't stand myself, how the hell will this child tolerate me? Just give up on me. Seriously. You deserve better.'

Like the finale of his stories, Aksh Soni unravelled in a fit of uncontrollable sorrow.

'Shhh Aksh. Shh. Let it out. Let it all out. Shhh. Shhh. The baby is going to love you, just like I do. Don't be scared. Shhh.' Sia held Aksh close and his head fell in her lap. The sadness subsided, drop by drop, as she stroked his hair. His breathing turned even and then he was asleep. She stayed up most of the night, holding his head against her womb, knowing the little, lost boy had finally come home to her, a grown man.

# 22A

To Karin,

'As she undressed her mind,
I saw the lashes of life on her scarred soul,
her heart veiled in layers of pain.
I tried,
But it was forbidden to enter inside.
She had shut the door.
It was to be opened,
nevermore.'

Slam.

'Towards the sanguine light, the moth was drawn,
even as he sensed it would be his last flight.
One dance was all he had pined for,
and then he was willing to be forever gone.'

Poof.

'The poet wept,
Not only because forevermore she left his bed,
But at the poetry she left, branded in his head.'

Finito.

Aksh

# EPILOGUE

*T*hree years later...

'Mamma, the courier has a parcel for you!' yelled Shanaya.

Karin signed the receipt and turned around the parcel. The address seemed unfamiliar. Not another fancy wedding invite! She tore the cover and her heart started racing.

### The Melancholy of Manhood
#### by
#### Aksh Soni

No note. Nothing. Only the book.

She felt dizzy with the nostalgia. It was like a past life that had illicitly surfaced, clawing its way through time.

She thumbed through the pages of his unreleased novel. The temptation was too powerful to resist. She cancelled lunch with the 'gals' gang. In the confines of her bedroom, she could hear Aksh speak in every line, that she absorbed voraciously. A stunning, mature Aksh. His technical finesse wed to verbal mastery, in one blinding explosion of creative catharsis. His book was, in a word, brilliant.

Then she saw it. The dedication.

*'To those tufts of nothingness that complete us, as they pass by irrevocably, but leave behind a trail of tranquil reminder. In them, lies the transitory lodestar who taught me to cleanse my quill of cynicism in the endless inkwell of undefinable emotions.*

*To my wife, Sia, for her unflinching support to a sometimes unhinged me and for understanding my silence more than my words.*

*And*

*To my daughter, Arzoo, whose radiance eclipses all other creations of mine.'*

She bit her quivering lips to hold back the deluge of tears threatening to burst forth and shatter her composure into smithereens, as she saw his handwriting etched on the page, reaching across the searing chasm that divided them.

*Dear Karin,*

*Keep seeking and your story will meet you halfway, on the horizon where imagination and inspiration become one.*

*Fond regards,*

*Aksh Soni*

She sat still for an interminable period of time. Then, as if in a trance, Karin began to type. The moment was here. This was it. Her untold tale.

### 'Akshar—The Divine Dance of Words'
### By
### Karin Mehra

*Chapter 1*

*There was a man I met once, though only in fantasy. A messiah sent by the muses, who set me gently adrift the babbling brook of my awaiting book....*